DANGER TASTES DREADFUL

BERNIE AND TISH

BEN LANGHINRICHS

Clean Reads
GREAT STORIES. NO GUILT.
www.cleanreads.com

Danger Tastes Dreadful
by Ben Langhinrichs
Published by Clean Reads
www.cleanreads.com

DANGER TASTES DREADFUL
Copyright © 2018 BEN LANGHINRICHS
ISBN 978-1-62135-789-6
Cover Art Designed by AM DESIGNS STUDIO

For Julie,
my best friend, sharing the grandest adventure of all

_____

TROLL, INTERRUPTED

TO A TROLL, OR AT LEAST ONE OF THE TROLDFOLK LIKE BERNIE, trouble had a spicy cinnamon smell. He recognized it because a faint whiff always hung around his best friend, Tish. But the odor that wafted out from the deeper woods wasn't faint at all. He bent down and sniffed. His feet, green and sweaty, stank as usual, but this was worse. Frowning, he ran his stubby tongue across the path, getting a large mouthful of forest junk.

He gagged on the bitter taste. Bernie knew he'd tasted that bitterness before, but where? Before he could figure it out, he felt a beetle wriggling on his tongue. Spitting out the gross, slobber-covered twigs and leaves, he caught the beetle and munched on it, enjoying its crunchy texture.

Bernie stopped, mouth hanging open. That bitter flavor was the taste of danger! Trouble and danger? He twisted around but didn't see anything unusual. No footprints. No looming shadows. No beady eyes peeking out from behind a bush. Nothing moved except the leaves, which danced in the breeze. He relaxed. Maybe it wasn't danger after all.

CRACK!

The loud noise echoed through the forest. Bernie jerked

upright. He knew what he should do, what his dad would do. He should investigate, find the trouble, and stop the danger. After all, trolls were tough and feared nothing.

At least, that's what his dad always said, but Bernie didn't feel tough. His knees wobbled, his ears lay flat, and his heart hammered like a woodpecker in his chest.

Hurrying back down the path with all the haste a troll could manage, he repeated to himself, *smells like trouble, tastes like danger, sounds like thunder*, over and over, trying to keep it straight in his head.

When he reached the old stone bridge, Bernie stopped to catch his breath by the weeping willow tree. It hung out over the Garlknack River, trailing its branches in the slow-moving water. On a normal day, Bernie liked to drop sticks on one side of the bridge then run to the other side to see them reappear, but today was not a normal day.

Leaning over the edge of the bridge, Bernie opened his mouth to call to his mum but then snapped it shut again. He remembered his father's disappointed look when Bernie came home scared the last time. Even worse, he remembered his mum turning to his dad and saying, "Don't worry, he's still young."

Not this time, Bernie thought, though his heart still pounded.

A long, sharp whistle carried across the river from the meadow on the far side of the bridge. Bernie saw his father's quick grin before it disappeared behind the tree he was dragging out of the woods.

His mum's knobby green head popped out from under the bridge, small brown eyes squinting in the bright sunlight. "Back already, Bernie? Is anything wrong?"

"No, mum," Bernie said over his shoulder before trotting across the bridge and over the meadow. He stopped as his dad threw down the tree. The trunk was splintered. It was a treetop really, broken off a large elm. "Where'd you get this, Dad?" Something about the treetop bothered him, but he couldn't think what.

"I heard it fall. Must have been rotten, but it was too good to pass up." His father pulled at the branches and grinned as they snapped off. "Nothing better than breaking things on a sunny day."

Bernie knew he couldn't tear off the bigger branches, but he yanked at a smaller one on his side which came off with a satisfying crack. He laughed and tore off another, while his dad climbed up and jumped on the trunk, splitting it again.

After a few minutes of fun, Bernie and his dad collected some of the bigger broken sticks and carried them across the bridge to where Bernie's mother stood smiling. Bernie's father dumped his bundle by the side of the path, and Bernie dropped his own branches on top. By winter time, the sticks would be dry enough to burn to keep the cave warm.

"Hullo, dear." Bernie's father and mother rubbed noses together as they always did. He looked away until he was sure they were done.

"Did Bernie help you find wood today?" his mother asked, her arm looped through his father's.

Bernie bit his lip so he wouldn't growl. "I was out by myself," he said in defiance before his dad could answer. "I'm old enough."

"Course you are," said his dad with a grin. "Did you smell anything strange?"

"No, did you?" Bernie asked, a little too quickly.

"Nope, same old woods. No bears, no bobcats, and especially, no people."

Bernie shivered. People were bad news, almost twice the size of trolls and always cutting down parts of the forest or shooting guns at anything that moved. Fortunately, no people had been seen in the area for many years. Bernie didn't like that he lived under a bridge made by people, even if long ago, but his mum and dad felt comfortable there. Anyway, it was better than living in a scratched-out cave in the Hollows and fighting with other trolls all the time.

Bernie wondered whether he should tell his parents about the danger after all. What if it was people? Or a bear?

"Is lunch ready? I'm starving." His dad's voice interrupted his thoughts, and then Bernie's stomach rumbled loudly. All three of them laughed.

Maybe later, Bernie thought. *I'll tell Tish about it first.*

"I have newt stew all ready," Bernie's mum said, smiling. "Now, hurry, before it gets warm." She shooed them both down below the bridge.

"I'm going over to Tish's after lunch," said Bernie as he ducked under the edge. *Tish always knows what to do with trouble*, he thought. *Of course, that's because she's usually causing it.*

Crossing his legs and plunking down on the rough dirt, Bernie took the bowl from his mother. Thick and oily, the stew made his toes tingle with anticipation, but before he ate, he stirred it carefully with his finger. The small newts wriggled away, but he ignored them.

Then he saw it. Reaching in, Bernie pulled out a thin green stem. "Mum, you put dandelion stems in the stew again. You know I hate them."

"Eat your stew and stop complaining," his dad said, a tiny newt's tail poking out between his teeth. "You won't even notice them."

Bernie grimaced. The newts were good, but he was careful to pick out each dandelion stem, so the food was warmer than he liked by the time he got to the bottom of the bowl.

When Bernie finished, he grinned as he saw his father lying against the back wall, snoring. His mum held a finger to her lips. "Leave him be. Your dad needs his sleep. Maybe you could take a nap, too," she said, yawning and lying down beside his dad.

Trolls liked their naps, but Bernie was in no mood. He couldn't stop thinking about the strange smell and taste and even more about the loud crack. Something big was out there, he knew it. He hoped it wasn't a bear, but there was only one way to find out.

"Mum, I'm going over to Tish's." He shook his mother to make sure she heard, but after she grunted and rolled over, he gave up. It didn't matter if his mum or dad knew he'd left. What mattered was telling Tish, finding the danger, and proving he wasn't a coward.

2

STORM RISING

TISH LIVED WITH HER GRANDMOTHER IN A CAVE BEHIND THE waterfall. It wasn't a very big cave, and it wasn't a very big waterfall, but Bernie liked to visit. He and Tish had been best friends ever since she defended him when Grokko said Bernie feared his own shadow.

As Bernie reached the waterfall, a gust of wind sent twigs and leaves swirling. Clouds dashed across the sky, pushing and shoving against each other. He hoped the weather wouldn't get worse before he could show Tish the danger.

"Tish? Are you there?" Bernie shouted, pushing his face through the waterfall to be heard over the bubbling downpour, and soaking his head in the process.

"Come in, Bernie," Tish's grandmother called out in her wheezy voice. Granny Mac, as she insisted everybody call her, was grey and wrinkled. Even her warts had wrinkles, and Bernie had to be careful not to stare.

Tish always said Granny Mac was not as old as she looked. She must be right. No troll could ever be as old as Granny Mac looked.

Careful not to look down at the drop below, Bernie held his

breath and jumped through the waterfall. He shook off the water and wiggled his ears to clear them out. "Is Tish home?"

"She's out searching for stones for her collection. I don't know where we'll put them."

Bernie laughed. Shelves lined each wall, holding everything from tiny, polished pebbles to lumpy rocks as large as Bernie's head. He remembered to be polite and not say that normal trolls didn't make thing like shelves. After a quick "bye" to Granny Mac, Bernie ducked out of the other side of the waterfall to tell Tish about the troublesome smells.

Outside, Bernie stopped and scanned the hillside. Tish and her Granny were Huldrefolk, hill trolls, and hard to see if you didn't know just where to look. He could call out, but he liked it better if he could spy her without help. Finally, he noticed a movement near the water. *Found her!*

Tish sat on a rock, polishing a stone with her shirt. One strand of straight black hair hung down over her left eye. As she concentrated, she would push it out of the way, only to have it fall back.

Bernie hardly even noticed Tish's hair anymore, though he knew it bothered the other trolls. Huldrefolk had hair on their heads and grey skin instead of green. Weird! Nobody ever said anything to Granny Mac, of course, but some of the trolls teased Tish that she looked more human than troll. Dumb, since people weren't grey or knobby at all.

Holding the stone up, Tish inspected it with one eye shut. Then, she closed that eye and opened the other, examining it once more. Finally, with a brief shake of her head, she tossed it over her shoulder.

"Hey, watch out," cried Bernie, as the stone bounced off his arm. It didn't hurt, but it startled him.

"Sorry," Tish said without looking up. She said sorry a lot. "I'm glad you came over. How about this?" She reached into a small bag and pulled out a smooth black pebble with a fancy design like a spider web.

Tish carefully placed the stone on top of a skinny pile of rocks which wobbled but didn't fall. "I'm making a *langis*. Granny showed me how."

Bernie admired the stone, but asked, "What's a *langis*? I've never heard of that before."

"It's a word from an old language Granny knows. Something hill trolls used a long time ago, I think. A *langis* is a pile of stones you leave as a message. There's supposed to be all sorts of special messages, but I only know this one."

"What does it mean?" Bernie asked. It looked like nothing but a pile of rocks to him.

"It means 'I was here.' You can use it to mark a trail, and it won't get washed away."

Bernie nodded, then stopped in surprise. He thought for a moment Tish had burped, but this was sweeter, like butterscotch. He leaned close to the pile and another butterscotch burp popped in his left nostril. "Are you hiding something? It smells like a secret."

Tish shook her head, but her eyes twinkled.

Bernie poked at a flat stone near the base, and the whole pile crashed down. Tish growled, but Bernie ignored her and held up the flat rock. It had an angry face scratched on the flattest part. "This is from Grokko's cave!"

Tish laughed. "I took it while he was sleeping."

"But, Tish, he'll never figure out where he lives. He needs the stone to know which cave is his."

Tish snorted. "He deserves it. I passed him in the meadow yesterday, and he pulled my hair."

"You have to put it back. He's going to be so angry."

"I will, I will." Tish grinned. "Or maybe I'll put it in front of Toosha's cave. Boy, will she be surprised if Grokko walks in on her while she's eating. She already thinks he steals her grubs."

Bernie groaned and shook his head, then remembered why he'd come. "Wait, I forgot to tell you. I smelled trouble on the path, something big and dangerous, but my parents weren't interested."

"Let's go," cried Tish, leaping to her feet. "Maybe it's a dragon! I've always wanted to see a dragon."

Bernie wasn't sure dragons were real, but kept his mouth shut.

Granny Mac fretted and fussed, warning them about the approaching storm, but she finally let them go once they promised not to stand under any trees that might get hit by lightning.

The sky danced with distant flashes. Bernie and Tish stopped and listened. When they didn't hear any thunder, they went on. As Granny Mac liked to say, "Lightning isn't frightening if you wonder, *Where's the thunder?*"

They passed the fork, which led off toward the stone bridge, and walked all the way up to where the path entered the woods.

"How much farther until we get to where you smelled the dragon?"

"I'm not sure." Bernie looked for the bare patch where he'd licked the ground and tasted the danger. "I don't think it's a dragon. I'm not even sure dragons are real. But anyway, I smelled it right up there, or somewhere close by." Wind had scattered leaves and twigs across the path so nothing seemed familiar.

Tish scanned the undergrowth, probably hoping a dragon would pop out at them. The branches rustled and shook in the heavy breeze. Tish pointed at a tree off in the forest with its top broken and dangling. "Maybe a dragon ran into it," she said.

Even if dragons were real, Bernie didn't think one would run into a tree. "Smell the air," he said, raising his stubby nose and sniffing loudly.

Tish raised her nose too, black hair falling back over her ears. After a moment, she shook her head. "There might be something, but mostly I smell the storm coming." As she spoke, a flash of lightning crossed the sky, followed shortly by a rumble of thunder.

"Here, try the ground." Bernie licked a swath of ground, and swirled the bark and leaves in his mouth. The bitter taste was even stronger than before. "Come on, try. You can taste the danger for yourself."

Tish raised her eyebrows, "I'm supposed to taste *danger*? Bernie, you know I can't do that."

"Oh, sorry." Bernie found it hard to believe any troll couldn't taste something as bitter as this, but Huldrefolk were odd and couldn't smell or taste some of the things Troldfolk could.

Tish sniffed the air anyway. Her face fell. "Aren't dragons supposed to breathe fire? I don't smell any smoke or ash. It's probably just a bear." She kicked the ground. "There are dragons, you know. Granny says there are. She says they live in the Far Mountains, along with other horrible things." She peered about under the trees. "We have to search harder, that's all. We might find tracks!"

Bernie smiled faintly, glad she wasn't mad at him. He shivered at the thought of a bear, but didn't want Tish to see him scared, so he walked ahead of her into the woods. They checked the trunk of the broken tree for claw marks and the ground for tracks, but found nothing.

Bernie stopped. "Is the wind getting louder?" The trees swayed, and it was much noisier than when they walked up the path. From far off to the left, they heard a loud crash, like a tree falling.

"What was that?" asked Tish, staring off into the forest.

Bernie could barely hear her over the wind which howled around them as if angry it had been caught. "I don't know, but we'd better go home."

Tish hesitated, then nodded, and they started back down the

path. Trolls don't run if they don't have to, but Bernie and Tish walked faster than before.

A brilliant flash of lightning startled Bernie, and he squeaked, but the sound was lost in a crack of thunder, which followed closely after. Now, Bernie made himself run, feet slapping against the path. After a couple of minutes, he turned his head to see if Tish was all right, but she wasn't there. He couldn't see her anywhere in the gathering darkness.

"Tish!" Bernie called out, but the wind whipped away his words. The sky hung dark and heavy over him and made it difficult to see. Bernie scrambled back in the direction they'd come, wondering where in the gloom she could be. As he searched, rain started falling and more lightning streaked across the sky, followed closely by heavy rolls of thunder. He squinted through the murk, and finally as the lightning flared, saw Tish huddled under a large sycamore.

Bernie hurried toward her. "Tish," Bernie shouted when he got close to the sycamore, "you have to get away from there. Granny Mac said not to go under a tree."

Tish didn't say anything, but beckoned frantically to him to come closer. He started forward, but glanced up. What he saw made him forget all about the tree. An enormous shape stood outlined against the sky, and when it moved, the ground shook.

Bernie dove toward the trunk next to Tish. "What is that?" he whispered, not daring to raise his eyes again. Any answer would have been drowned out by the heavy roll of thunder following another brilliant flash of lighting. As the echo in his ears faded, Bernie heard a sharp crack directly above them.

The sycamore groaned and creaked, louder and louder. Bernie snapped his head up. The tree seemed to be falling toward them. "Watch out!" he cried, and grabbed Tish to drag her away. He was not much bigger than she was, but trolls were strong. Half carrying and half dragging, he ran as fast as he could back toward the path.

There was a gigantic roar as a major limb broke off the sycamore and crashed down, landing with a wallop beside them. A large branch whipped against Bernie's arm and knocked him off his feet. It would have broken a person's arm, but trolls were tough. He and Tish tumbled across the ground, rolling up against a boulder near the path.

"Tish, are you okay?" he cried, pulling himself upright. The rain poured down, and there were more tremendous rumbles as if the lightning and thunder were angry they had missed their mark. Bernie stared everywhere up in the dark, but the shape had disappeared.

"What was that?" Bernie asked. "It was huge."

Even through the rain, Tish's eyes shone with a mixture of fear and excitement. "Giants!"

3

DANGER OVERHEAD

BERNIE SAT BACK ON HIS HEELS. "GIANTS?" HE'D HEARD OF GIANTS, but thought they were made up to scare young trolls into behaving. He'd certainly never expected something taller than a tree.

Tish nodded. "I saw them. Two giants, maybe more, stomping and crashing through the woods. They were so big." Tish shivered and hugged herself. Bernie put his arm around her. He looked about fearfully. The sky was lighter than before, and he could see a few trees with broken tops or gashes where limbs were missing.

After a couple of minutes, Tish jumped to her feet. "We have to warn Granny."

"And my parents," said Bernie, standing as well. "I didn't tell them about the danger!"

They made their way back down the slick wet path, checking the sky and the undergrowth on each side. They didn't see any more giants or any sign they'd come this way. The only lightning came in distant flashes, though the wind had grown and swirled around them, throwing up leaves and sticks, so it was difficult to walk.

Bernie wanted to take the fork back toward the bridge to let his mum know he was all right and tell his parents about the giants, but Tish pulled him toward the waterfall. He decided to get her back to Granny Mac and then go home to his bridge when she was safe. He pushed through the wind and debris until they got to Tish's cave.

The waterfall cascaded down in angry sheets, spray and foam billowing out in all directions. To make matters worse, the rain started again, heavier than before. Bernie and Tish had to hang onto the protruding rocks to make their way through the pounding water, but they were so wet they didn't care.

"There were giants," Tish shouted into the cave, but nobody answered. "Granny?" She ran to the other end of the cave and then back to Bernie. "Where is she?"

"Maybe she went looking for us." Bernie looked back out at the turbulent waterfall. "She might think we went to my bridge. We should go there." His heart beat hard, and he found it hard to breathe, but he knew he had to stay calm for Tish. Thinking about his parents and the safety of his bridge helped a little.

Tish grabbed his arm. "We need to go find her. She... she might be worried about us." Wiping at her eyes, she leapt out through the torrents of water. Her excitement had died down, and now she just looked scared.

Bernie hurried after her, though he stepped carefully and breathed a sigh of relief when he was through. The pounding rain made it difficult, but Bernie fought his way after Tish. Mud sucked at his feet when he slipped off to the side, but the path itself was still firm.

Suddenly, Bernie grabbed Tish by the shoulder. "Stop. What was that?"

Tish opened her mouth to reply, but then snapped it shut as the ground rumbled under her feet. "They're close," she said.

Bernie didn't have to ask what she meant. "Come on. We have to warn Mum and Dad." He grabbed Tish's hand and pulled her along. As they neared the fork, the heavy rain let up, and the sky lightened some, but the rumbling and shaking continued.

A tall tree lay split in two across the fork in the path, which led off toward Bernie's bridge. They climbed over without saying anything, but Bernie's heart pounded at the sight.

On the other side, Bernie and Tish ran, jumping over small branches and puddles left by the storm, not saying anything. The roar of the storm-flooded Garlknack grew louder, until they turned out of the forest and stood in front of the stone bridge, or at least where it should have been.

The bridge lay in jagged pieces. One large section rested in the river, which ran high above its banks and thundered against the half-submerged stones. Another part of the bridge sat lodged next to the path in front of them. The weeping willow lay uprooted along the bank of the river, still trailing sadly in the rushing current.

"Down!" said Tish, pulling Bernie off the path where he stood staring at the destruction.

Across the river, three huge men strode toward them, the ground shaking harder with each step. They held their arms out, and it took Bernie a moment to realize they were carrying something in their hands. No, someone. "They've got trolls," he said to Tish, "but I don't know who. Can you see?"

"Bernie, we have to hide." She pulled him back further into the underbrush. Barely seconds later, the giant men stepped into the river as if it were nothing, and then out again onto the bank near Bernie and Tish. As they walked, they scanned the ground. "What if…?" Before Tish could say more, a giant foot crashed into the bushes nearby, shoving the branches hard against the trolls who were thrown to the ground.

Moments later, the giants were gone, striding off through the forest. The rumbles sounded more distant until the giants disappeared from view. Beyond them, Bernie saw the distant mountains, but nothing more.

Rushing to the edge of the river, Bernie tried to call out to his mother and father, but he couldn't get a sound out. He jumped down and landed hard among the collapsed pieces of the bridge. Shattered stones blocked the entrance to his cave. Sticking his head past the broken rocks, he squeaked out, "Mum? Dad?"

Tish climbed down beside him and started tossing loose stones out of the way. Bernie saw what she was doing, and moved any he could lift, heaving them away from the hole. When they got to an especially large boulder, the two trolls pushed and shoved until the boulder fell into the swollen river, which rushed by only a few feet away from the blocked entrance.

At last, Bernie squeezed into the cave, finding his voice and calling out for his mum and dad. There was no answer. The hole was empty. Bernie climbed all the way back, hoping he would find his mum and dad hiding up high where the water could never reach, but they weren't there. He backed out and slumped down on the bank, barely feeling Tish's hand on his.

"The giants must have them." A tear ran down Tish's cheek.

"Maybe mum and dad made it to the Hollows. They could have gone for help." Bernie stopped when he saw her face. "Maybe Granny Mac went after them."

Tish slapped her tears away. "You're right. We must find a way across the river. If they're over on the far side, they'll be worried sick about us."

Bernie stared back at the broken bridge for a moment, then nodded. He didn't want to think what the giants might do to his mum and dad if they weren't in the Hollows. "We can get across the log bridge. Come on." The log bridge wasn't a proper bridge at all, but a tall tree that had fallen across a narrow part of the Garlknack downstream from Bernie's home. Young trolls used it as a shortcut, though their parents often warned them it wasn't safe. Trolls don't swim, they sink, so falling in the river could be deadly.

Bernie grabbed Tish's hand, and the two of them walked

together as best they could. Many large branches lay across the way, though whether the storm or the giants had knocked them down wasn't clear. Tish and Bernie climbed over some branches and around others. By the time they reached the narrow part where the tree had lain across, Bernie was not surprised it had washed away. The storm must have been a terrible one.

Tish kept staring at the tumultuous waves, as if the tree might reappear if she looked hard enough. "What do we do now?" she asked in a trembling voice. Tish was almost never scared, but somehow, the raging river between them and any other grown-up trolls shook her more than the giants, and her fear made his stomach hurt and his eyes blur.

Standing there staring, the two heard a faint shout over the roar of the water. Across on the other side, they saw Madulsa, a grizzled old troll who could often be found in a clearing near the Hollows, sipping from a hollowed-out gourd and telling wild, unlikely tales. Bernie remembered his dad shaking his head and muttering about trolls wasting their lives.

"Didja ... fierce ... giants?" Madulsa shouted. Bernie had to strain to hear, and still missed most of the words.

"They broke our bridge into pieces," Bernie called out, cupping his hands to try to be heard over the pounding water. "How can we get across the river?"

Madulsa shrugged and pointed at his ears. Tish and Bernie tried shouting together, but it was clear the old troll couldn't hear anything. After a moment, he waved his hands as if to stop them and shouted back. "... took ... trolls away." He pointed across the water, though Bernie couldn't tell what he pointed at.

Tish tried again, "Did they take Granny?"

Bernie yelled as loudly as he could. "Did they take my parents?"

Again, the old troll shrugged. He pointed again behind them, then turned away and stumbled back toward the forest and wouldn't respond to their shouts.

4

ONE SMALL STEP

Bernie stared across the water, then turned to Tish. He blinked away his tears. Inside, he felt empty and his gut ached, but he also felt something different. He felt angry. "It's not fair. We have to get them back."

Tish gaped at him. "Get them back from the giants? How? We don't even know they're still alive." She clapped her hand over her mouth, eyes widening and brimming with tears. She sat with a thump.

"They have to be." Bernie rubbed his fist across his own eyes and stood up. "I don't know how, but we're going to rescue them." He looked at Tish, who still sat dazed, her shoulders shaking. "Or at least I am. You can stay here if you want."

Tish scrambled to her feet. "Stay here without Granny? No way. I'm coming with you."

Bernie stopped. "But where are we going? I don't even know where the giants came from. We can't just walk toward the mountains."

Tish brightened. "Granny says the giants live on Mount Dreadful." She turned and pointed off to the distant mountain

18

range whose tallest peaks could just be seen above the forest. "It's supposed to be the biggest of them all."

Bernie looked, then turned back to the path, talking as he did. "Mount Dreadful?" The name terrified him. "Then I guess that's where we have to go." His stomach churned, but not like hunger. More like the storm yesterday. He didn't want Tish to see him scared. He had to be tough and fearless, like his dad said.

"We don't have any choice," Tish said. "We'd better hurry too, before the giants do anything to your mum and dad and… and Granny."

Bernie closed his eyes and concentrated until his ears stood straight up. What would his mum and dad tell him if they were here? They'd say to be prepared for anything. Opening his eyes, he said, "We can't go without supplies. There's no way we can catch up with giants, no matter what we do, so we have to be ready to follow them all the way." Bernie shivered and moved closer to Tish as they headed back to the waterfall.

Bernie kept looking over at the mountains in the distance. He didn't know how far away they were or how to climb Mount Dreadful when they got there. Trolls don't climb mountains, though perhaps hill trolls do. He looked at Tish. Even if they did find a way up Mount Dreadful, he had no idea how to rescue his parents, but he knew he had to try. He bumped Tish's shoulder with his, glad at least he didn't have to face the journey alone. She didn't look any happier, but she bumped his shoulder back.

Behind the waterfall, Tish emptied the rocks she'd been collecting out of her sack. "We can carry some food in here," she said, then stopped. "But what else will we need?"

Bernie looked at her blankly. He tried to imagine what you might need to take on a rescue mission to fight giants. He shrugged, "Who knows? I've never gone on a journey, any journey." The enormity of their task struck him, and he sat on the floor.

Tish stared at him, then shook her head. "Don't give up, Bernie. They're depending on us."

"You're right," Bernie said, taking a deep breath. "How about blankets to keep us warm?"

Tish rummaged through Granny Mac's things and found two blankets. She also found a metal canteen and a warm hat, which she put on and pulled down over her ears. Bernie snickered, but when Tish glared at him, he stopped. At least it covered her hair.

Outside, the two trolls looked at each other. Neither had ever traveled far from home, and certainly never without grown-ups. "Which way should we go?" Bernie asked. "We could follow the stream above your waterfall. My mum says it comes from the mountains, but it isn't straight. I don't know how much longer that would take."

"We could cut across the plains," Tish said, "but Granny says they are hilly and dry." She held up the canteen. "This is all the water we can carry. I think we have to follow the Lillygusset." At Bernie's puzzled look, she said impatiently, "I mean our stream. It has a name, after all. Anyway, if we go upstream, we'll have to get to the mountains eventually even if it isn't straight."

They looked at each other, not sure how to decide. Finally, Bernie took a deep breath and said, "You're right. We should go by the, er, the Lillygusset. That way, we'll at least have water."

Tish looked grateful he'd decided, but it made Bernie's stomach hurt a bit. He hoped they'd made the right decision.

Bernie and Tish climbed the path alongside the waterfall and started off up the stream, making their way through the birch and pine trees. When there was a clearing, Bernie looked off at the mountains, but they didn't seem any closer.

The waters of the Lillygusset roiled and roared by. It was much smaller than the Garlknack, but the storm water still overflowed the banks in places. When Bernie and Tish came to these spots, they had to pick their way past the marshy, mushy ground. By late afternoon, they were exhausted and irritable.

"Can't we stop?" Tish groaned as they trudged up a steep hill. The trees closed in on them, and long vines hung every which way, making the climb even more difficult. "I don't like the look of these woods. Maybe we should go around."

"No," snapped Bernie, more sharply than he intended. "We can't risk getting lost." He knew what his father would say. Trolls are tough and fear nothing. Well, it was about time for him to be tough and fearless and show Tish she could depend on him to get them where they were going.

"We can stop when we get to a clearing," Bernie said, "maybe at the top of this hill where we can get a look around."

Tish held back, looking at the bank of the stream through the underbrush, but Bernie forged on and she soon followed. He stepped between two trees and brushed a hanging vine away from his face. The steep slope and jumbled branches made it difficult to walk, but Bernie wanted to get to the top. Soon, he could see sky through the trees. They must be near the highest point. He stepped forward while turning his head to tell Tish, but instead found himself grasping wildly for something to hang on to as the ground crumbled beneath him.

"Tish!" he yelled. He tumbled down into the icy cold water, which closed over his head in an instant.

5

TISH ALONE

Tish heard his cry and rushed to where he'd been a moment before, but caught herself before plunging down after him. She could see now how the water had worn away the hillside, leaving only a thin layer covered by leaves and brush. "Bernie!" she cried out through the gap where he'd fallen, before she glimpsed Bernie's green feet sticking out of the water as the current carried him off.

Without pausing, Tish crashed back down the hill the way they'd come, ignoring the underbrush and vines, which whipped at her face and caught at her feet. She tripped on a root and fell but got up and kept running. "I'm coming," she called, though she had no idea how far down the stream he might have been swept. An image of her waterfall downstream crossed her mind, but she pushed it away along with the branches.

At the bottom of the hill, Tish forced her way to the bank of the Lillygusset, squelching through sticky, cold mud. When she reached the water's edge, she stared up and down for any sign of her friend. She called out and listened, but all she could hear was the stream. Tears welled up in her eyes, when suddenly she heard a faint wail. Out in the middle of the stream below where she stood, Bernie clung to a rock, though little more than his ears and the knobby tip of his head stuck out. Tish stared at him. She couldn't swim, and the water was much too fast anyway. She needed to find some way to reach him.

"Hold on," she cried out across the water, hoping Bernie could hear her. She squelched back through the mud. She saw a long branch, but Bernie was too far away. As she walked, she slipped and reached out to grab at one of the trees but instead found herself hanging on one of the dangling vines.

Shaking the vine, Tish let out a whoop. It disappeared far up into one of the taller trees that hung out over the mud. She put all her weight on it, but the vine held firm. Tish could see several trees with vines, including some closer to the water. She let go and made her way back to the edge. She had to go a little further upstream to find a good vine. She yanked on it, and it came partway down and then stuck.

Turning to the water, Tish tried to throw the vine out toward Bernie, but it splashed into the stream less than halfway to him and then floated back along the bank. She tried again, but with no more success.

She could see Bernie had pulled himself a little further out of the water and was watching her. She waved and tried to throw the vine one more time, but still couldn't make it far enough. Frustrated, she sat and tried to think. Maybe there was a log she could float on or something else she could use. Upstream, a long straight birch tree had fallen and hung out over the stream, but it was anchored to the bank with a huge bunch of roots and dirt, and not even a grown troll could shift something like that. The woods thinned out downstream, so there wasn't anything there she could use.

Tish stood and stamped her foot. She picked up a little stick and threw it into the water where it made an angry splash and was swept away. Tish watched it go, and threw another in. As it too disappeared into the brisk current, she nodded. "Hang on, Bernie, I'm coming," she shouted across to him.

Grabbing the vine, Tish dragged it to the leaning birch tree. In general, trolls don't climb, but Tish knew she could do this. She was a hill troll, which should mean something. Though she'd never tried before, she pulled herself up onto the tree. It didn't budge, so she moved further out, hanging on to the vine with one hand and pulling herself along with the other. As she moved out over the stream, she looked down and quickly back up again. It made her dizzy seeing the water rush by, and she didn't want to fall. The branches grew thicker and the tree trunk more narrow as she moved out. A gust of wind rocked the tree. Tish clung to the limb, shutting her eyes so hard they hurt. After the wind passed by and she caught her breath, she shimmied further out.

Finally, Tish could go no farther. She wasn't quite as far out as Bernie, but it would have to do. Clutching the vine in her hand so she didn't drop it, she wound it one time around the trunk to keep it steady. There was still plenty of give, so she pulled the vine further and held it against the tree. When she thought she was almost level with Berne, she let the loose part of the vine go. The end fell into the water and snaked its way downstream. At its limit, the vine was only a little distance from Bernie's rock.

Bernie watched Tish make her way out on the tree, though he still didn't comprehend what she planned to do. When she wound the vine around the tree and dropped it, he understood and pulled himself up to sit perched precariously on the rock with water rushing by him on all sides. As the vine came closer, he grabbed for it, but it swirled away from him. It kept slithering back and forth in the current like an evil water snake, and while his fingers grazed it, he couldn't quite catch it. He waited one more time, then leaned out as far as he could and grabbed for it, when all of a sudden, he lost his footing and slipped. His last thought as he fell into the swirling water was to push himself off the rock toward the vine, so when he went under with water everywhere and his nose filled up, he felt the end of the vine between his fingers and clutched it with desperate strength.

———

As he spluttered to the surface, Tish gave out another whoop. She shoved at the loop of vine, and it slid a little way down the tree toward shore. Bernie tugged and swatted at the vine until he got his other hand on it. Clinging with first one hand and then the other, almost crying when the vine slipped a bit through his fingers, he pulled himself toward the tree. He didn't think he could climb it, but if he got close enough to shore he might be able to grab the branches.

Slowly, Tish pushed the vine down the tree trunk, breaking off any small branches in its way. When she reached a branch she couldn't break, she backed herself past the branch and grabbed the vine below it. This was harder, as Bernie's weight and the current pulled on her, but she managed to edge closer to shore. Now the slithering vine helped Bernie, who swung back and forth in the current until he was close enough to get a tentative footing in the shallow water.

Tish pulled and Bernie leaned, and finally he was able to clamber ashore.

Tish jumped off the tree and ran to Bernie, but he lay face down on the ground, coughing and spitting up water. She sat and thumped him on the back, and more water came up between his coughs.

When the coughing fit stopped, Bernie rolled over toward Tish. "I can't believe you. How did you figure out what to do?"

Tish's ears grew bright red. "It was nothing," she mumbled.

"You saved my life," Bernie said. Tish looked away, and he

stopped. "We need to find a place to sleep. Everything aches, and I am so tired."

"Me, too," said Tish as she helped him up. She held his hand as they made their way back through the mud and then trudged through the wooded area until they reached a meadow beyond. They didn't talk, but Tish guessed they both wanted to be as far from the stream as possible. After the last trees dwindled, with night approaching, they found themselves walking up a rocky hill neither had ever seen before.

Tish stopped at the top of the hill. All she could see was trees behind and hills covered with broken rocks and small brush everywhere else. "It's going to be dark soon," she said.

Bernie nodded. His face looked haggard, as if his eyes would barely stay open.

Tish started forward. "Let's go while we still have light. Take your time and look to the left while I'll look to the right. If you see a cave or overhang or anything, call out."

Bernie followed, stumbling and nodding. Tish glanced back at him, worried he might tumble and knock them both down the hill. Behind him, a flat slab of rock protruded from the hillside. "Bernie! What about that?" She tried not to yell at him, but she was tired, too.

Bernie flushed. "Sorry, I guess I missed it," he mumbled.

"Let's go underneath and make sure it's big enough for us." There wasn't much room, but it was dry. Exhausted, with feet aching, the two lay on the hard surface back to back. Tish kept still, thinking about the awful day. She heard Bernie's breathing slow and settle into a gentle rhythm.

Alone and worried about her grandmother, Tish let the tears come pouring out. For the first time since her parents disappeared and Granny took her in, Tish cried herself to sleep.

6

A SUDDEN DROP

A LARGE BLACK BEETLE WITH GREEN STREAKS ON ITS BACK SCURRIED across the ground in front of Bernie's one open eye. The sound of its skittering had woken him, and he watched as it hurried and stopped, hurried and stopped. Could the beetle taste danger like Bernie, or did it see the trolls and get scared? To it, they must seem like giants.

Bernie's stomach rumbled. The insect froze in its tracks as Bernie slowly reached out his hand. It trembled, watching his hand get closer, but seemed unable to run away.

The beetle was within his reach, and Bernie wanted nothing more than to pop it into his mouth and crunch it up, but he couldn't. He knew what it was to be that scared. "Shoo," he whispered, and nudged the terrified bug with his finger.

The beetle raced away, diving under some rocks scattered outside the overhang. Bernie watched it run, but then his stomach rumbled again. He sat up.

Tish rolled over and opened her eyes. "Where are we?" she asked, then sat up as well. "Oh, we're here," she went on. Bernie couldn't argue with that.

"We need to find something to eat," said Bernie. He didn't mention the beetle.

Nodding, Tish stood up and went to forage on the hillside. Bernie followed her. Bleak, rocky, and barren with only small plants peeking out from the dry patches of dirt, the hillside did not seem promising.

Bernie yanked on a small grey shrub. The roots held tight for a moment, then came free all at once, scattering dirt in his face. Bernie chewed on the tough, sour leaves. *Ugh!* Worse than thistle. Even worse than dandelions. He walked over to Tish and gave her the rest.

"Thanks," she said, but eyed the plant dubiously before chewing on it. The expression on her face made Bernie laugh, and Tish stuck her tongue out at him.

After the unsatisfactory breakfast, they started out again toward the mountains, but not before Tish made another *langis* on a flat rock near where they slept.

"Do you think anybody might see that and know to come find us?" he asked, letting a note of hope creep into his voice. It was lonely out in the wilds, and he couldn't believe the mountains were any closer no matter how far they walked.

Tish shook her head. "Probably not, but I think it's worth making them anyway."

"Why?"

"Well," Tish said, turning away from the distant mountains and looking back where they had come from. She waved a hand at the horizon behind them. "It's all the same back there. No landmarks like the mountain. I'm not sure we'll know how to find our way back if we don't."

Bernie bit down on a finger, staring back. He hadn't thought about the return, could hardly imagine it and assumed his mum and dad would know the way. He nodded, and they started off again.

After about an hour of walking, Bernie yelped as Tish pitched forward without a sound toward the dirt, hands outstretched. "Are you all right?" he asked, kneeling beside her.

Tish rolled over, grinning. Clutched between her hands was a large red salamander, wriggling like mad. "Got him," she said, her eyes dancing. She shoved the salamander halfway into her mouth and bit down hard.

While Tish happily chewed the front half of the salamander, she handed the tail end to Bernie. He was surprised it still wiggled, but didn't let that stop him. He popped the jerking red salamander butt into his mouth and chewed it slowly, savoring the taste.

Finished, Bernie plopped down beside Tish. "Thanks," he said. Tish smiled. They rested for a while, then stood up and continued walking.

On and on they went. The sun rose higher in the sky, and Bernie felt hot and tired. Not sleepy, but tired in his legs and back. Tish kept wiping sweat off her forehead with her sleeve, so he decided not to complain.

The hills grew steeper and the rocks bigger. Repeatedly, they climbed up one side of a steep ridge or hill only to slip and slide down the other. With the salamander a distant memory, and the occasional small plant a bitter substitute, Bernie and Tish struggled on.

"Heeeellllppp!" Tish's scream startled Bernie. They had made it over a tall, sharp ridge when Tish disappeared from sight, leaving only her scream echoing through the air.

Bernie stood for a moment staring at where she had been, then lay against the hill on his stomach and scooted up until his head hung over. On the far side of the ridge, a steep angle led to a deep crevice between the rocks. Narrow at the top, its smooth sides sloped down and grew closer together. He couldn't see more than a few feet down into the gloom. "Tish, where are you? Are you okay?"

After a groan, Tish's voice came back, echoing between the

sides so he couldn't tell where exactly she was. "I'm stuck. I fell down... and it's too narrow."

Bernie heard her grunting with exertion, and then a squeak.

"I can't reach anything with my feet, and the sides are too steep and flat. There's nothing to grab onto down here."

Tish's voice sounded desperate, and Bernie had to do something. "I am going around to the other side. It's lower down, so maybe I can reach you there."

He circled down past the crack until he could approach from the opposite side, but he still couldn't see Tish. He called, and Tish's voice sounded closer when she answered. Closer, and even more scared. She couldn't find a way to climb out, or even move from where she hung wedged in.

Bernie sat back. Rocks, large and small, covered the area. It reminded Bernie of the broken stone bridge and his parents, but he forced back his own tears. No time for that now. Instead, he scouted about for sticks, anything which might help him reach Tish. He wondered if there any vines out here, but all he could find was tiny shrubs like the yucky one he'd eaten earlier.

Going back to the edge, he peered in. Maybe if he hung down, Tish could grab his feet and he could pull them both up. "Tish, watch out for my feet. When I tell you, grab them and I'll pull you up."

Tish called up she would, and Bernie turned and backed up until his feet hung over the drop. Gulping, and wishing there were a better way, he slid backward and let his legs dangle. Gripping the edge, he lowered himself down, little by little.

"Grab my feet," he called out.

"I'm further down to your left," Tish said. "Move closer."

Bernie clung to the edge of the crevice. He could barely hang on and couldn't see how he could move left. Finally, he inched his fingers over, one hand at a time. He braced himself for the extra weight, but all he felt was the tip of Tish's fingernail scraping along his heel.

"I can't reach," Tish called out in a shaky voice. "Can't you get any lower?"

Bernie tried to stretch out. He held on with only his fingertips, but he couldn't get any lower. Finally, his arms aching, he pulled himself back up. "I have to go for help."

"And leave me here?" wailed Tish. "You can't do that. You'll never find me again. I'll die down here."

Bernie sat miserably by the side of the hole and reassured Tish he wouldn't leave her, he would find a way to get her out. "I'm going back to the top to see if I can see anything long enough to reach you. I won't go away. I promise."

Making his way back to the higher side of the crevice was hard work. At last, Bernie pulled himself up, but as he reached the top, his toe banged into a loose rock which popped into the air and fell down into the crevice with Tish.

"What are you doing?" Tish shouted. "That almost hit me."

Bernie didn't answer her for a moment. Instead, he pushed with his feet at the rocks and small boulders. There were many more than even Tish's rock collection back behind the waterfall. Perhaps he could make a huge *langis*. Maybe someone would see that. He picked up one large rock to find out how heavy it was, but it slipped and fell at his feet. He jumped out of its way, then gasped at the sudden minty smell. Opportunity. Leaning back over the edge of the crevice, he called down, "Hold on, Tish. I have an idea."

7

FALLING INTO PLACE

BERNIE STUDIED THE GROUND AND ROCKS, TRYING TO THINK. HIS plan might work, but maybe he'd mess it up and hurt her, and then he'd be all alone out here. If only he had somebody to talk to about it, somebody other than Tish. There didn't seem to be any other way to get her out, though he thought until his brow furrowed and his ears rose straight up. He hoped this would work.

After a few minutes, he heard Tish calling again. "What are you doing up there?" Her words echoed around the hole, but even so, he could hear the quaver in her voice.

Lying down and putting his head over the crevice, he called out, "I'm going to throw some rocks down the hole." At her frightened squeak, he reassured her he was going to try to fill the hole part way. "Maybe I can get enough to reach you, but you have to tell me if I am getting too close. I don't want to hit you."

"Be careful," Tish said. "I don't want to die down here."

Bernie didn't know what to say. Instead, he got a small rock and dropped it in some distance from where Tish fell in.

"You have to get closer than that," Tish called out. Her voice sounder braver now she knew what he was doing.

Bernie picked up a bigger rock, making sure it was not too jagged. Trolls are tough, but a heavy jagged rock would still hurt Tish if it fell on her. He went back to the crevice and dropped the rock in.

"Hey, one got wedged in here like me," Tish said. "Put in more like that, and maybe I can pull myself up."

Bernie picked up another rock and dropped it, only to have Tish howl. "Ow, ow, ow. Not so close. That hurt."

Bernie stopped and found a rock of a different shape than the others, with three pointed sides. He laid it down to mark the place where the first rock went in, so he wouldn't forget and get too close to Tish. Then he started making a good-sized pile after reassuring Tish about what he was doing.

Tish answered that she understood, but her voice fell off at the end. Bernie knew he had to hurry.

Carefully, Bernie picked up each rock and held it over the edge well away from Tish, close to the pointed marker rock. The rocks clattered down, and Bernie checked after each to make sure Tish was okay. No more hit her, though a few came near.

When Tish called out, "Stop!" Bernie ran to the side, thinking he had hurt her, but Tish called out she thought enough rocks were wedged in she might be able to pull herself up. After some huffing and puffing, she called out again. She was free, and her voice sounded far more cheerful.

After this, Bernie was even more careful, throwing down flatter rocks. After each couple of rocks, Tish piled them up before stepping back to let him throw more. When Tish's hand reached out of the hole, Bernie let out a whoop and grabbed hold. He pulled and she climbed, and soon she was out of the hole, her dirty, dust-streaked face grinning from ear to ear.

Bernie threw his arms around Tish and hugged her until she squeaked she couldn't breathe. When he let go, she gasped a bit and then grinned at him again. "You did it, Bernie. You figured it out all by yourself."

Bernie's ears grew hot. "It was nothing. I thought… you know, about your *langis*." He stopped, not sure what else to say.

"Well, I think we may have some ways to fight giants after all," Tish said.

"What do you mean?" Bernie asked, wondering what weapons Tish could be talking about in this barren place.

"I mean, maybe we have something special about us. I know, trolls aren't supposed to be smart, we're supposed to be tough and strong and fearless like your dad says. We're not supposed to make things or solve problems; we're supposed to break things and cause problems."

Bernie tried to figure out what she meant. Of course they were supposed to break things, they were trolls!

"But maybe we're more than that. When you fell in the water, I figured out a way to use the vine and the tree to rescue you. I made something, and it worked."

Bernie's ears lifted a little. What if Tish was right? He already knew she was clever at making things, even if she didn't like to admit it. "But what about me? I'll never be as clever as you are, and I'm scared all the time." He looked down at the ground, not sure he should have said that. Tish depended on him. He shouldn't say he was scared, but then again, Tish knew that.

"Well, maybe being scared isn't the worst thing," Tish went on. "When you tried to be tough and fearless, you pushed through the trees and fell in the water."

"I didn't mean to…" Bernie started, but Tish held up her hand to stop him.

"I know," she said, "but what about when I got trapped in the hole? You were scared, but it helped you slow down and plan a way to get me out. Most trolls wouldn't do that."

Bernie's ears rose a bit. "So, when trolls stomp around and are fearless, sometimes it makes the trouble worse?"

"Yes. When you smelled trouble and tasted danger, you could

have gone out and gotten killed by the giants, but you didn't. You came and told me."

"I should have told my parents," Bernie said miserably.

"Maybe, but at least you didn't get stomped on. Running into danger isn't always the smart thing to do."

"I guess not," said Bernie. His ears lifted higher into the air. He knew Tish was clever, even if she didn't like to admit it. What if being scared made him a little more careful, maybe even smart in a different sort of way. "When we left your cave, I was scared of going out on our own, but then I suggested we take supplies, and that was a good thing."

Tish grinned, "See, sometimes it helps to be a little scared. It makes you think ahead."

Bernie grinned back. Tish might be every bit as weird as the other trolls said, but maybe she was weird in a special way. Maybe he and Tish could figure a way to help his parents and the other trolls after all.

"Right now, we need to find a place to sleep," Tish said. "Being rescued is hard work!"

Bernie laughed, then heard a scratching noise above them. He was startled to see a thin, grey hand appear over the top of the ridge and grasp hold of a jutting bit of rock.

8

APPROACHING MOUNT DREADFUL

As the two trolls stared and backed away, a series of grunts echoed from behind the ridge before a head appeared, a familiar head. Bernie hesitated, unable to believe his eyes, but Tish ran forward. "Granny," she called out. "Where? How?"

The old troll didn't reply, but kept clambering over the ridge and finally down beside Tish. She dropped the pack she was carrying and gave Tish a great hug. "My sweet girl," she wheezed. "Oh, my dear, sweet girl, you're safe."

After a moment, Bernie ran over and joined in the hug. The three held each other for a couple of minutes before Bernie stepped away. He looked at Granny Mac. "What about my mum and dad?" he asked. "What about the giants?"

Granny Mac put an arm around Bernie and patted his back. "When I arrived at your home, I talked to your parents and told them about the *jötunn*, what you call giants. We agreed I'd warn the other trolls in the Hollows, and they'd go find you, but I'd barely gotten across the bridge when the giants came stamping and pounding. They tore the bridge apart with their hands. One giant caught your mum and dad trying to get out from the other side, but the others kept breaking up the bridge and

36

tossing the pieces everywhere. I stayed still, so they didn't see me."

Her eyes clouded over, and she took a deep breath. "I didn't know what to do. I was on the wrong side of the river, and I didn't know how to get back to you. So, I went to the Hollows, but all the trolls were missing except Madulsa. He said most of them got away and were hiding."

"How did you cross the river? We couldn't find any way."

"It took me a while," Granny Mac wheezed, sitting. "Finally, I found a loose log, pushed it into the river and jumped on."

Tish gasped, her hand over her mouth.

Granny Mac patted her hand. "I've done worse, dear, back when I was young. Anyway, the log bounced and rolled in the current. I must have looked one sorry, wet troll before the log wedged itself up against the far side of the river."

Granny Mac stopped for a moment, and wiped away a tear. "I had to go all the way upstream again, but couldn't find anybody near the bridge. I went back to our cave, but there was no sign of you there. "

"We must have missed you. We thought the giants had taken you too," Tish cried out. "We didn't mean to scare you."

"Well, you did scare me, quite badly. At first, I worried the giants had taken you, but there were no footprints or broken trees near our waterfall. At last, when I went back into the cave to think and make a cuppa, I saw you'd taken supplies. You wouldn't have done that if you were captured, so I realized you must be on a rescue mission."

Bernie and Tish looked at each other. Rescue mission. It sounded almost foolish when Granny Mac said it aloud. "We had to do something," Bernie said, afraid Granny Mac would laugh at them.

"Of course you did. I'm proud of the two of you," Granny Mac said, "although you might have been better off if you had taken more food." Turning back to her pack, she pulled out three small packets, wrapped in leaves. She carefully unfolded the leaves and scooped a handful of the contents to each of the younger trolls.

"Grubs," cried Bernie. He picked up several and started dropping them into his mouth, two at a time. He never remembered anything tasting so good. After gobbling down his whole packet of grubs, he turned to Granny Mac. "Thank you."

"Now," said Granny Mac briskly, "we'd better find a place to spend the night."

Bernie sniffled, though he wouldn't let himself cry.

"What's the matter?" asked Granny Mac.

"Are you... are you going to make us go back?" Bernie asked.

"Go back?" Granny Mac's eyes narrowed. "Of course not. I'm joining your rescue mission, not stopping it. We are going to get your parents, and no giants better stand in our way."

Her tiny, winkled face was so fierce, Bernie stepped backward. Then he understood what she'd said, and he threw his arms around her. "Thank you. I have to save my parents."

Granny Mac's face softened and turned serious instead of fierce. "I shouldn't promise too much, Bernie. Giants don't usually hurt trolls, but they don't usually steal them away either. I don't know what we'll find when we get to Mount Dreadful, but I promise we'll do our best."

Bernie nodded. His throat had a lump in it he couldn't swallow, so he didn't say anything else.

The three travelers climbed down the hill with its terrible crevice after Tish told Granny Mac the story. Bernie's ears burned, and he tried not to listen, but it made the lump go away.

Off that hill, they searched for a safe place to spend the night. The sun was much lower before they found a burrow, dug out from the side of a hill by some animal long before.

"We'll sleep here," announced Granny Mac, after she had examined the cave carefully, but he and Tish were already lying down. Her words were the last thing he heard before falling asleep.

Bernie woke to Tish prodding his arm. "Wake up, sleepyhead." Bernie opened his eyes. Tish grinned down at him, all smiles now her grandmother was with them. Bernie was glad, but a little jealous. Why couldn't his parents be safe as well? He rubbed his nose on his arm, wiping his eyes as he did. Then he stood and helped Granny Mac store the blankets she had covered them with during the night.

"Your granny is amazing," Bernie whispered to Tish as the old troll picked up the heavy pack and marched down the slope. "She carries a pack I could barely lift, and she tracked us through the woods and over the rocks and hills."

"I told you she wasn't as old as she looks," whispered back Tish. "Come on, we have to move now or she'll be all the way to Mount Dreadful and we'll still be standing here."

Bernie and Tish took off after Granny Mac, who moved quickly despite her size. She led them off to the right, and soon they walked out of the stony hills and into a meadow, where the walking wasn't so hard.

In the meadow, it was easier to find bugs to munch. Bernie even found a small, but delicious, garden snake, which he shared with Tish. Granny Mac refused any, saying she could manage her own meals.

With his eyes on the ground, spying for beetles, Bernie didn't notice how much closer the mountains were until they stopped for a rest and *a cuppa*, as Granny Mac described a thick bitter drink she poured from a canteen attached to her pack. She insisted they all have some.

Bernie didn't like the taste much, but the drink filled him up in a way little else had. He wondered what was in it, but decided he wouldn't ask. Grown-ups had strange ideas about what was good for you.

While they rested, Granny Mac pointed to the mountains

looming near them. "We call them the Far Mountains, but those who live nearby call them the Avergills."

Wondering exactly who or what lived near the mountains, Bernie shifted closer to Tish and Granny Mac. The mountains seemed wild and very, very tall.

"Mount Dreadful is that large mountain over there," Granny Mac continued, pointing to a steep mountain with a white rim near the top.

"Why is it white up there?" asked Tish.

"Snow," answered Granny Mac. "It gets colder the farther up you go, and when you get high enough, there's snow." She stared at the peak. "I hope we don't have to hike up so high, but I don't know where the giants live. I guess we'll have to try and find out."

At the thought of the cold, forbidding mountain, Bernie closed his eyes and wondered if they could really climb it. Even if they did, how were they going to fight giants taller than the treetops?

Granny Mac stood and brushed off her legs. "We'd better get closer to the mountains before dark. See the forest between us and Mount Dreadful? We'll try to get to the edge, so we can make a fire tonight to keep any prowling creatures away."

Bernie and Tish looked at each other. Tish shivered and chewed on her knuckle, eyes darting back and forth. Bernie took her hand and squeezed, and then they hurried together to catch up to Granny Mac.

Dusk had settled onto the land, casting long shadows that bounced along with them, when they finally came upon the first grove of pine trees. Beyond, the deeper forest made a dark line between them and the mountains. Granny Mac held up her hand and halted them.

"Let's not go into the forest until tomorrow. We don't know what lives there, but this patch of trees should do nicely for tonight." She spoke with confidence, but Bernie noticed she sounded wheezier than she had when they rested earlier. He didn't know whether she was tired, or as worried as he was about the animals living in the woods.

Late that night, Bernie woke. The moon filtered through the trees and scattered shadows around their small campsite. Wind blowing through the branches set the shadows to dancing. One shadow did not dance with the others, and Bernie watched to see what it might be. He couldn't taste any danger on the cool breeze, so he kept watching.

At first, he saw nothing, but then the shadow turned and as it melted into the dark, Bernie recognized the quick flash of a fox's tail. Though foxes posed no real danger to trolls, Bernie scooted closer to Granny Mac and Tish and closed his eyes. He hoped there wasn't anything bigger than a fox out there in the dark.

STAIRWAY TO NOWHERE

WHEN BERNIE WOKE AGAIN, GRANNY MAC HAD A SMALL FIRE going. Propped over it was an iron pan, which Granny Mac stirred occasionally. Bernie's parents never cooked his food, and he wasn't sure what it would taste like, but it certainly smelled wonderful.

Bernie yawned, scratched his stomach, and climbed out from under the blanket. Tish popped her head out when he moved, and they walked over to the fire together.

"I've got a special treat for you this morning." Granny Mac's eyes twinkled. She pointed to the pot on the fire.

Bernie leaned over, peering into the thin brown speckled liquid. "What is it?" he asked.

"Wait a minute, you'll see. Keep watching."

Tish squealed, "I saw a tail. Oh, Granny, did you catch a mouse?"

"Not just one," said Granny Mac, clearly pleased with herself. "There are field mice all through the grass here, and I caught three plump ones. In a few minutes, we'll have a proper meal."

Bernie licked his lips. He could almost taste the mice and hoped cooking them didn't ruin the flavor. Granny Mac puttered about, preparing the meal, and Bernie couldn't help thinking how out here in the wild world, she didn't act so ancient. Also, she didn't wheeze as much. He shook his head. He'd never understand grown-ups.

The meal tasted delicious, though Bernie let it cool down before he would try it. Then, after he finished, Bernie turned to Mount Dreadful. Stark and barren, it towered in the distance. Even if they made it up, how were they going to get his mum and dad away from the giants?

"Don't worry so much." Granny Mac chucked Bernie under the chin. "My gran told me, *worry about things when you get to them, not before.* You worried about the cooked mice, and that turned out well, right? We'll get up that mountain, but not until we get to it, and we'll find a way to rescue your parents, but not before we find them." She gave him a quick hug, and then moved off to load up her pack.

The forest stood between them and the mountain range, so Granny Mac led them to the edge where they searched for a way through the thick, jumbled branches. In the forest near Bernie's bridge, the trees grew farther apart with lots of clearings and empty space. This forest did not leave any room for walking through.

Rather than enter in such a dense tangle, Granny Mac took them along the edge of the forest. They still had a long walk ahead past the other mountains to get to Mount Dreadful itself, and she told them she hoped they'd find a spot nearer to the mountain where the branches would let them through.

They walked for hours, but the dense forest never gave way. At last, sometime after midday, they were as close to Mount Dreadful as they could get without entering the woods.

"I'll go first, but you two stay close behind me." Granny Mac pointed ahead. "There's a little room at the base of the trees, so we'll stay low."

Bernie wasn't sure he would fit where Granny Mac ducked in,

but he crouched down and found he could shove the branches and brambles aside with his shoulder. It was slow, difficult work which scratched his back, and not in a pleasant way. They stopped frequently to rest, but it never seemed long enough.

Fortunately, once they had made it about halfway through, the trees thinned out some, and there was room to walk upright. Bernie wondered if the barrier was natural or whether somebody had made sure the forest line would be hard to break through.

It didn't matter. They stepped out of the edge of the forest. Mount Dreadful loomed ahead, tall and menacing. Bernie craned his head and stared up the side of the mountain.

"How will we know where the giants live?" Tish asked. "I don't see any caves from here."

Granny Mac shook her head. "I don't know. No troll in recent memory has gone up Mount Dreadful, or at least none who have come back." She stopped, perhaps realizing how terrible that sounded. "We'll find a way. It isn't like many trolls have tried, either. The giants must have a way to climb the mountain, and we will follow that."

"We'd better start looking," Bernie said, trying to sound brave, though he doubted he fooled them. "Should we go left or right?"

After a few minutes of arguing back and forth, they decided to go right. Granny Mac heaved the pack onto her back, but she let Bernie lead. The forest line wandered back and forth, so sometimes they walked among trees and sometimes in the open. It would have been clearer on the mountain, but Granny Mac said walking on a tilt was hard, so they agreed to stay back from the edge.

Every time the trees retreated and they had a clear view, they stopped and searched the mountain for clues. On all sides, the slopes were steep and barren. Bernie stared up the mountain, seeking out some path giants might use or some sign they lived here at all. What if the giants didn't live on Mount Dreadful anymore, and they'd come all this way for nothing? "Are you sure the giants live here?" he asked Granny Mac. "I don't see caves or buildings or anything giant size, and I can't smell anything but forest."

"I'm sure," Granny Mac said grimly, but she wouldn't explain more. "Keep looking."

Finally, when he'd almost given up, Bernie saw something. "Wait, up there on the mountain. Smoke."

Close to the peak of the mountain on the far left, a ridge jutted out, and beside it rose a thin column of smoke, though frequent gusts of wind made it swirl and disappear. Through sheer luck, Bernie caught sight of it during a moment of calm.

"Good work," Granny Mac said. "Now, watch the mountain closely. Giants can't fly any more than trolls can, so they must have a way up."

They kept walking, watching the mountain through gaps in the trees and slowly circling toward the ridge Bernie had spotted. As if to stop them, the trees drew closer together. Granny Mac took the lead from Bernie and started in toward the lower slopes of the mountain.

Tish saw it first. "Up ahead," she called out in excitement. "There's a stairway leading up."

The stairs did not go straight, but wound back and forth up the side of the mountain. In places, the steps weren't visible at all, but they would start again a little further on.

Tish's face fell. "But they don't go anywhere. They stop halfway up. They don't go anywhere near the smoke."

Granny Mac scratched her head, and pulled on a wisp of grey hair. At last, she said, "All we can do is go up and see if there is something beyond the stairs. They can't go nowhere."

Granny Mac sounded less certain than she had before, but Bernie said nothing. The sight of the stairs made his heart pound. He hated heights the way most trolls did, and those stairs were far higher than anything he'd ever imagined anything could be. But his parents must be up beyond those stairs somewhere, and he would have to brave them even if the idea made everything from his ears to his toes shake.

10

ONE GIANT STEP FOR TROLLS

THEY STILL HAD A LONG WAY TO GO TO REACH THE BASE OF THE stairs. The terrain was rough near the mountain, with boulders and dense thickets of brush. They had to make their way around and climb in and out of gulches. After walking until Bernie felt like his legs would give out, the trolls stopped to rest and eat some lunch. Bernie longed to give his feet a break, but the thought of his parents made him restless.

Granny Mac pulled some dried worms from her pack. Bernie chewed on them to stop his stomach growling, but they tasted like boredom, which has almost no flavor at all. He gazed at the steps, trying to figure out what bothered him about them.

"Granny Mac," he said suddenly, "those stairs were made for giants."

She nodded.

"But that means they're much too big for us." Bernie blushed. Obviously, the steps would be big. He hoped Granny Mac wouldn't laugh at him.

She didn't. "I've been worried about that while we walked, but I think even if we can't use the steps, we can follow them up the mountain. With the way they go back and forth, the giants who made them must have found some less steep places. If we stay close to the steps, we can take advantage of those less steep places ourselves."

"What if the giants use the stairway while we're climbing up?" Tish asked. "There isn't any place to hide up there. I think we should climb straight up the mountain. We can see where the steps lead even if we don't follow them, and we would save lots of time by not going back and forth."

Granny Mac examined the mountain. "I suppose we could," she said. "I don't think the giants use the stairway often, but it might be safer. What do you think, Bernie?"

Surprised she would ask him, Bernie paused for a minute. He looked up the mountain and then over at the stairs. "I think Tish is right," he said with some hesitation. "If we followed the steps, we'd know we were going the right way, but I'd hate to meet those giants out in the open. If we went up the mountain from here, we could stop in some of those clumps of trees if we needed to hide."

Granny Mac's eyes went from Tish to Bernie and back, but then she nodded. "Sounds reasonable to me."

Bernie gulped, and Tish's mouth hung open as well. With all her camping tricks, it was obvious Granny Mac had done lots of hiking in the wild, but she was willing to do what they suggested.

Picking up the pack, Granny Mac headed toward the mountain. Bernie shrugged, grinned at Tish and followed along behind her, trying to keep up.

The ground beneath them got steeper as they went. Granny Mac aimed them upward and at a slight angle so they would go close by one of the tight curves in the stairway. Bernie thought she might be giving them a chance to change their minds and follow the stairway if the other way was too hard.

The going was slow, but steady. Bernie found it hard to keep his footing on the steep slope. He worried he might fall backward down the mountain if he wasn't careful. At least the ground was stable and easy to grip with his fingers and toes. At one point, Tish slipped on a loose rock and tumbled down until she caught onto a stunted pine tree growing on the mountainside, and managed to stop her fall. After she made her way back to Bernie and Granny Mac, they were all even more careful, so their progress was quite slow.

Climbing over the last steep part before the step, Bernie stopped and stared. Tish clambered up behind him and asked why he'd stopped.

"It's beautiful," he said, his voice barely above a whisper.

Granny Mac climbed up beside him and gaped at the wall along with the two of them. "Giants made that?" Tish said in astonishment.

Unlike the rough-hewn steps they expected, intricate lines covered each stone. Though ancient and worn, every step had elaborate carved designs which rose as tall as three trolls standing on top of one another.

Ornate patterns with whorls and flourishes decorated the edges, but the vertical side facing the step below it told a story in pictures, so a giant walking up the steps would see story after story, or maybe the same story linked together. Bernie thought it might be some sort of history of the giants.

Granny Mac sat and stared at the steps, her brow furrowed. Bernie and Tish sat beside her, waiting to hear what she might say about it. "I don't know much about giants," she admitted. "Giants haven't bothered us in a long, long time, and all I've ever heard is tales of huge men and women whose feet will crush anything they walk on. No troll has gotten close enough to learn more, nor wanted to, but there are stories…"

She stopped and scratched her chin. "I find it hard to believe giants who were capable of creating that would steal away trolls, but these steps are old and weatherworn, so maybe they were made by an ancient race of giants. We need to be carefulThere may be more to these giants than I thought."

Bernie walked over to the closest step, fascinated by all the work which must have gone into them. Why? He traced the whorls with his finger, trying to imagine anyone spending the time it would take to make these fancy carvings.

A cry from Tish startled him. He ran to see where she pointed. It was the flat part of the step where the story was carved. On it, two giants stood together pushing a crank of some sort, though what it might turn, he couldn't imagine. Tish nudged his arm and pointed lower. A tiny figure stood near the giants, though a little off to the side. "It's a troll!" exclaimed Tish.

Bernie, Tish and Granny Mac studied the carving for any clue why the troll was there. They couldn't tell if the giants were aware of the troll, but he wasn't hiding. Bernie noticed the troll had hair on his head like Tish and Granny Mac, so he must be a hill troll. There seemed nothing else to discover.

All three trolls agreed they should follow the stairs for a while and see if they could learn anything more from the stories inscribed on them. Bernie hoped they might find something that would help when they finally found the giants, if indeed they did still live on Mount Dreadful. He didn't share with Tish and Granny Mac how his heart sank when he saw how big the giants were in the carving compared to the tiny little troll. How could the three of them fight giants ten times their size?

11

OF MICE AND TROLLS

AFTER RESTING AND EATING A FEW MORE DRIED WORMS, WHICH Bernie decided he *did not* like, they started again. They soon discovered they couldn't follow the stairs even if they wanted to, as the ground alongside the steps was worn and steep, so they had to continue as before climbing straight up the mountain. Bernie looked back as the steps turned farther away, wishing he could see the stories on them and wondering whether more trolls appeared.

The three aimed for the next bend in the stairs, if only to have a goal, but it was too far to reach before nightfall. As dusk fell, they veered off to the left where a scraggly tangle of trees offered some shelter and protection from view.

They couldn't find any mice this high up on the mountain, but Bernie and Tish dug until they found a few grubs and live earthworms. A cold wind blew across the face of the mountain, and the three huddled together under their blankets and wished for a nice, warm cave.

Bernie heard Granny Mac's whistling snore and Tish's slow, steady breathing, but he had trouble falling asleep. Assuming Granny Mac was right, his parents were somewhere on that mountain, if they were still alive. For the first time since he and Tish had taken off on this journey, he let himself think about whether his parents might be dead.

They couldn't be. He wouldn't believe it, but the idea settled into his mind, and he couldn't get rid of it. Why would the giants take his parents? Was it possible they looked at trolls the way he looked at field mice?

If so, why had they never bothered the trolls before? Granny Mac told them she hadn't heard of a giant who paid any attention at all to trolls in years and years and years, so why now?

While he lay still, trying hard not to think of all the possibilities, he heard a low whooshing sound overhead, like the river overflowing with spring melt near his bridge. A moment later it was gone, but Bernie peeked out from under the blanket and saw a shadow against the sky. It swooped around the mountain and disappeared.

What was that? Tish and Granny Mac were asleep, so he couldn't ask. He thought about waking them, but decided there was nothing they could do, and all of them needed sleep for the climb ahead. Bernie watched the sky for a while longer but saw nothing else. Finally, his exhaustion overcame his worries and he fell asleep.

"It was huge and flew right over us," Bernie told Granny Mac and Tish when they got up in the morning.

"You should have woken me," said Granny Mac, her face furrowed even beyond its usual wrinkles.

"I would have, but it was gone before I had time," said Bernie, a little annoyed he hadn't and more annoyed she criticized him about it. Worry about his parents was starting to nag at him all the time, and he felt grumpy and tired.

"It was probably an eagle," said Granny Mac. "They live in the mountains but don't bother with trolls. We are too big to carry off and too small to frighten them."

Tish said nothing, but her eyes shone with eagerness. Bernie wondered what she was thinking, but soon his mind was occupied with climbing the steep slope. There were more loose rocks as they went up, and if you stepped on one, you could fall, so they climbed with hands and feet gripping anything solid.

They were nearing the end of the stairway, or at least what they could see of it. Far above them, Bernie saw the jutting ledge where he had spotted smoke before, but it looked far out of reach, and the height made him dizzy. Granny Mac watched for movement above them, but Bernie and Tish kept their eyes on the ground at their feet.

When they reached the final curve in the stairway, Granny Mac said they would follow it up, even if it was difficult. The incline was steep, and she warned them to lean in to the mountain so they wouldn't fall backward and roll down the slope.

It was hard climbing from step to step, but it was a great relief to be able to rest on the flat surfaces. Granny Mac watched above constantly, always checking for places they could hide if any giants emerged from the mountain, but they saw and heard nothing. The stories near the top were wilder and more mysterious. They saw no more trolls, but there were other creatures they could not identify.

As they climbed beside the top step, they came to a sudden narrow plateau, invisible from below. On the plateau was a road. Peeking out over the step, Bernie got his first good look at a real giant since the brief glimpses of the ones he'd seen stomping off with his parents. Halfway down the road, a huge man sat on a low bench, low to the giant at least. Bernie was sure he could walk under the bench without bending over.

Bernie stared. The giant didn't look much like a troll at all, more like a person except five times the size. He had hair on his head, but not like Tish or Granny Mac. It was all over, and there was some on his face as well.

The giant was terrifying, but somehow reassuring as well. Bernie had grown more and more afraid they would make it up the mountain only to discover the giants were not there.

Then the giant stood, shielded his eyes against the sun and looked around. "Get down," whispered Granny Mac, and they all ducked behind the corner of the step.

A few minutes later, Granny Mac peered out and said the giant was walking away from them. Bernie gulped at the tremendous strides the giant man took toward the mountain before ducking his head and entering an entrance of some sort at the end of the road.

"That is where we need to go," Granny Mac said, her voice grim but determined. "Let's hurry before any others come out."

The road was made of large stones, like the steps, but without any designs. The stones were large enough they could walk alongside them and find places to duck into if any giants looked out, but if one walked down the road, there was little cover. It made for slow travel, but the earlier sight of the giant made walking on the road itself seem terrifying.

It took almost an hour to walk the length of the road, and by the time they drew close to the entrance, the sun cast long shadows behind their backs, and the chill in the air made Bernie shiver. He was surprised to feel warm air blowing out from the cave, carrying with it an earthy smell and a faint hint of smoke.

Bernie stopped and sniffed the air, then leaned over and licked the ground near the entrance. The bitter taste was unmistakable. He spat on the ground to get the harsh flavor out of his mouth, then said, "It's the danger I tasted before. It's in there."

ENTER THE MOUNTAIN

ON THE LONG WALK DOWN THE ROAD, BERNIE HAD TRIED TO imagine a cave big enough for giants, but he couldn't believe the monstrous cavern beyond the entrance. It rose high above their heads, the ceiling lost high above them in the gloom. A road sloped downward into the deep inky darkness, not made from stones as the road outside, but a path which seemed carved out of the mountain itself. Torches hung on the walls and illuminated the path, but no light would have lit up that immense space.

Bernie wondered if his parents were below them somewhere in the murky depths and how he might find them. He closed his eyes for a moment, thinking of their smiling faces. A tear slid down his cheek, but he wiped it away. Taking a deep breath, he opened his eyes and walked past the entrance to the top of the road. Tish and Granny Mac followed close behind.

Tish spoke with awe in her voice, "The whole mountain is hollow. What is this place?"

"It must be *Jötunheimr*, home of the giants," Granny Mac said, whistling softly. "I've heard stories about it but thought it was a myth. I don't think even giants could dig out a cavern like this. This must be an old volcano or some other trick of Mother

Earth. I wonder where all the heat comes from." The warm air rose from below, but there were no apparent fires or furnaces to explain the heat.

As their eyes adjusted, they could see far below them what appeared to be a town, though little could be seen except patches of light illuminating passages between the buildings.

In the town, giants could be glimpsed when they walked near the torches. Two stood still under one patch of light, but most seemed to be moving about and working. The town looked a little like the ones people build, except the giants were much bigger than people, and the road, which ran through town, appeared to be one spiral leading to a central plaza.

"How will we find my parents?" asked Bernie, gazing down. He hadn't expected so many giants.

"We'll have to sneak down to the edge of town," said Granny Mac. "If we stay in the shadows, we won't be seen."

Bernie hoped she was right. The trolls hurried away from the entrance to a pool of darkness away from the closest torch.

There were many shadows, which made it easy to avoid being seen but difficult to avoid tripping and falling. Walking quickly was impossible, because in the dark areas not lit by torches, they had to inch forward, feeling with their toes.

Part way, they had a scare when the giant who had been outside came back up the road, his footsteps making the ground beneath them vibrate. Huddled in a pool of darkness away from the torches, they tried not to move or even breathe. Bernie wondered how well giants could see in the dark.

After a few heart-stopping minutes, the giant was past. He walked to the top of the road without looking back, and soon went out of the cave entrance.

As they crept forward again, making slow but steady progress down, more of the town became visible. Bernie counted over thirty houses before he got dizzy and had to stop. It was difficult to be sure where houses started because some lights were outside on the road and others were inside the houses, which didn't seem to have roofs. Bernie guessed with the warm air and no rain or bad weather, roofs were not a necessity.

"Look." Granny Mac pointed to a building near the center of the spiral, much larger than the others. In front of the building, a giant in a uniform stood by the door. "A guard if ever I've seen one."

"Would giants need a guard for a couple of trolls?" Tish asked. She looked at Bernie quickly, then away again.

"We don't know whether they took more trolls from the Hollows," Granny Mac said, still watching the town. "They could be anywhere, but I think that's where we should start."

Darting from shadow to shadow, they continued down the road. Each time, before they moved, they watched for guards or anyone who might be looking up at the road.

Bernie watched for guards as well, but he was also watching an open area where four giants sat together. There was something odd in the way they sat and talked, but he couldn't put his finger on what it was.

As they drew level with the tops of the houses, the road narrowed. From above, the spiral road had been clear enough, with the large guarded house visible in the center. Lower down, it was impossible to see more than the closest street. Granny Mac suggested they walk between the houses to get to an inner part of the spiral. It would be darker and there would be more places to hide. "Fewer giants," she whispered by way of explanation.

The houses of the giants were round. Some were simple circles and some more like ovals. Bernie was surprised to see the doors to the houses didn't face the street, but rather off to the sides or even out the back. It meant they would have to be careful when walking between houses, as a giant might walk out a door and surprise them.

It also became clear some houses did have roofs, while others had none or only parts of roofs. Suddenly it came to him. "It's a ruin," he whispered to Tish. "The giants are living in the remains of an old city."

Granny Mac nodded thoughtfully. "You're right, that must be it. I couldn't figure out why some of the buildings had gaps in the walls."

"But if they could build houses like this before, why can't they fix them now?" Bernie asked.

"Maybe these giants don't make things, same as trolls, or at least most trolls," Tish said. "Maybe it was different giants who made this town. It does look old, ancient even."

"Perhaps so," Granny Mac said, "though there's no way to be sure. All I know is, they are big enough to squash us if we aren't careful, so let's worry about that right now."

13

BUMP, RATTLE & ROLL

THEY WERE CLOSE TO THE FIRST HOUSES, WHICH TOWERED OVER them. Bernie saw a couple of giant women on the road, chatting together. He motioned to the others to stop in the shadow.

It felt like forever before the women said their goodbyes and went off in separate directions. As soon as they were gone, Granny Mac gestured for Bernie and Tish to follow and hurried across the road to the shadow of the first house. The torch from the street did not reach around the curved wall, so they walked slowly around the perimeter, watching for a doorway.

Before they came to one, they scurried across a narrow yard to yet another house. This time, they were not so lucky. As they circled around, they came upon a stoop with a door open behind it. On the stoop sat a baby giant, as large as four trolls on top of each other. It pushed a ball around, but stopped at the sight of them.

For a few moments, the baby stared at them, and they stared back. Nobody moved until the toddler stood up, shoving its ball aside. The huge toy rolled off the stoop, bounced in the air, and crashed into Tish before careening off into the dark.

Bernie gasped, afraid to move until the giant baby teetered

59

away inside, calling out, "New toy. Want one. Want one." Its wails grew louder, but the trolls were too busy to pay much attention. They ran to Tish, who lay still on the ground. She stirred and moaned, before finally sitting up. Bernie helped her to her feet, though she hunched over and coughed hard after he did. He wanted to get them away before the baby's mother came out to find out what the *new toy* might be.

Fortunately, Tish got her breath back soon and was able to walk. Nothing appeared to be broken, and they traveled on to the dwindling wails of the baby.

The next house they reached appeared abandoned. The door was open and crumbled, and there was no sign of life. The trolls went in the doorway and rested out of sight, but left again in a few minutes, driven out by the gloomy darkness.

"Who knows what might be in there," said Tish, wincing a bit as she talked. "I wonder if there are giant rats."

Granny Mac shushed her, and they went on. As they reached the next spiral of the street, they found a giant leaning his chair back against a house, sound asleep and snoring. They waited for a bit, then ran as fast as they could, which wasn't very fast, across the vast street and into the shadows on the other side.

House after house, street after street, they made their way inward to the town center. As the spiral tightened, they encountered the street more frequently, but it also narrowed as they approached the middle.

When at last they reached the edge of the center of town, they stopped in the shadows and rested. Granny Mac scouted out the open area. It was impossible to distinguish the large building they'd seen from above now, as all the buildings loomed far above them and looked equally huge. It took a few minutes before Granny Mac pointed out the guard pacing in front of a doorway about a third of the way around the circle to their right.

"We'll go behind the houses and see if there is any way to get in without the guard seeing us," said Granny Mac. "If not, we may have to watch until he takes a break or is busy with something else."

This plan didn't work. It was impossible getting to the back of the houses, because most joined together in the tightest spiral around the center. They had to take chances and run in front of the houses, under the torches that lit up the street.

By the time they had made it to the edge of a wall shortly before the long central building, they were exhausted and nervous. When they peered around this wall, they saw it was a market of some sort, with many giants bustling in and out carrying sacks of food. Bernie almost sat and cried.

"How are we supposed to get past all those giants?" he asked Granny Mac.

She shook her head, which Bernie took to mean she didn't know either. "Let's rest for a while before we try," she said, and to Bernie her voice sounded weary and older than before.

As they crouched in the dark, Bernie watched the giants. There seemed to be two burly ones who carried various sacks and boxes into the market, while everyone else entered empty handed and walked out with smaller loads.

He also noticed the market was mostly open air. Around the edge was a wall, which must have been low for the giants but was almost three times Bernie's height.

While he watched, the two men he saw taking goods into the market came huffing down the street, carrying a pallet between them loaded high with smaller boxes and sacks. They stopped and dropped the pallet near the trolls, kicking up dust that made them all rub their eyes.

As the giants stood panting and wiping at their brows, a young giantess greeted the two and offered each an earthenware mug. They thanked her and sat on the pallet, drinking from the mugs. The giantess stayed and talked with them, standing so close to the trolls they cowered back in the shadows. At one point she touched the blond giant's arm, and they locked eyes for a moment and then quickly glanced away. As they did, Bernie smelled a sharp burp of butterscotch, but shook it away. Whatever secret the two giants had, it didn't matter to the trolls.

Bernie gestured to the pallet. "If we could get on, they'd carry us in."

"It's too dangerous," Granny Mac said. "They'll see us."

Tish said nothing, and Bernie caught a whiff of cinnamon over the dust and sweaty smell of the market. Before he could say anything, Tish crept out behind the giantess, hiding from the men's sight. Bernie couldn't see what she was doing, but held his breath, sure Tish would be caught. He hoped giants weren't any better at seeing the Huldrefolk than he was. Granny Mac took his hand and squeezed, though neither dared even whisper.

A few moments later, Tish dove back into the shadows when the men stood up and handed the giantess their mugs. "Get ready," Tish said. As she did, the giantess moved toward the market, but she'd only made it one step before she stumbled and fell, dropping the mugs.

The men jumped forward to help her. Tish poked Bernie and said, "Now." The three trolls raced to the pallet as the men helped the giantess up and she dusted herself off. They hid beneath the sacks and waited.

"What did you do?" Bernie asked Tish.

Tish giggled. "I tied her boot laces together."

A moment later, everything shook and rumbled as the giants lifted the pallet. Bernie felt himself almost crushed as the sack he hid beside shifted.

After several tortured minutes, the pallet landed with a bone-shaking crash. On one side, Bernie saw huge feet, but on the other were more boxes and sacks, but no giants.

Poking Tish, he motioned toward that side and scrambled off. Tish and Granny Mac followed. They were in a storage area at the back of the market. They could see giants walking around, but none came close to them.

"Now what?" asked Tish.

"We're on the far side of the market," Bernie said. "We need to find a way out this side."

They scouted and watched for their chance. An entrance stood part way down the wall, but the number of giants made it impossible to get there undetected.

They sat and waited, surrounded by the smells and sounds of the giants, the thud and scraping of boxes and sacks being dropped, opened, and parceled out.

For the longest time, they saw no opportunity to get to the door. After a while, they talked quietly about whether they should try to sneak into a bag to be carried back out of the market again, but there didn't seem to be any way without going farther into the store, which seemed too risky.

They were stuck in the market of the giants, close to where Bernie's parents might be, yet unable to get there.

14

SEPARATED

THEY WERE SITTING, FRUSTRATED BUT UNABLE TO GET OUT OF THE market, when Tish exclaimed, "Look, in the window."

Bernie turned around. From where they sat, hidden behind a sack, they could see over the wall to the next building. Unlike most of the buildings, this one had windows set into the wall, with bright lights inside.

Inside the second window from the front, he could see a cage. Inside the cage, a bear paced back and forth. It was a long way off, but he was sure it was a regular-sized bear like the ones who sometimes went through the woods near his bridge. To think, only recently, a bear seemed like the scariest thing he might find in the woods.

"Why is that bear in a cage?" Tish asked her grandmother. "Could it be a zoo?" Troll parents often told their children stories about the zoos in which people kept animals of all sorts locked inside cages for other people to watch.

"It might be," said Granny Mac thoughtfully. She stared up at the bear which snuffled around its cage before settling back down on its haunches. "I wonder if that might be..." She didn't go on.

"Might be what, Granny?" Tish asked.

"If it's a zoo," she explained, "that might be why the giants took Bernie's parents and the others."

"They put my mum and dad in a zoo?" Bernie asked, outraged at the idea.

"We won't know until we get in there," Granny Mac cautioned him, "but at least it would mean they are alive."

Bernie flinched. He had been so intent on getting to his parents, he had forgotten they might have been hurt or killed. "We've got to get in there," he said in a low, urgent tone. "We've just got to."

Before anybody could respond, a loud voice echoed from above their heads. A giant leaned over the shelf under which they were hiding, his hand groping near them. "Move this lot outside, it's needed for the banquet," boomed the voice.

The shelf shook, and flour dust rained down on the trolls. Granny Mac grabbed both younger ones by the hand and pulled them back moments before a huge crate crashed down next to them. Its slats were made of tree trunks, and inside lumpy cloth sacks reeked of old onions and fresh dirt.

"Quick, into the crate," she ordered Tish and Bernie, and they all ran to the nearest gap. Tish and Granny Mac fit through easily, but Bernie stuck for a moment before they pulled him in.

Back up in the air they went, but the lumpy sacks proved far worse than before. The onions inside shifted and settled, mostly onto the trolls. The smell was overwhelming, making Bernie's eyes tear up.

"Ouch!" he said as a particularly heavy lump landed on his back.

"Quiet," whispered Granny Mac, although Bernie heard both her and Tish groaning too. Fortunately, the giant carrying the crate was singing a song about the ocean, and didn't seem to hear the trolls.

Outside the market, the giant turned, and walked back along

the wall. *He's going to take us inside the big house*, thought Bernie, but instead the giant dropped the crate with a tremendous thud onto the street near the doorway.

All three trolls were aching by this time, but pulled themselves out from under the lumpy bags, gasping for fresh air, to look out through the slats. There was a good deal of bustling about by several giants, although it was hard to tell them apart from the vantage point of the crate.

"Look, there's the door. It's open," said Tish, pointing out through one of the gaps.

Bernie and Granny Mac crowded around. The door was close enough to catch a glimpse into, but it would be impossible to get across that distance with all the giants walking around.

"We'll have to wait a bit and see if they either take us inside or go away," said Granny Mac.

Then, as if they were not sitting in a giant town surrounded by danger, she sat and pulled more dried worms from her pack. Bernie ate his quickly. He decided hunger made even dried worms taste better, though the smell from the bags behind them made the worms taste like onions.

After they had sat for a bit, the trolls were startled into diving under the sacks by a bugle call that rang out in the crowd and reverberated off the far cavern sides. Bernie crept back to the edge of the sack and peeked out. His heart thudded in his chest, but he had to see what was happening.

All the giants gathered in a circle around a white-haired giant who looked almost as old as Granny Mac. By his side, Bernie saw a young bugler.

"This is our chance," said Granny Mac in a low urgent voice. "Come, quick, while they are looking the other way."

Tish grabbed Bernie's hand, and they squeezed through the slats. Behind them, they heard a stentorian voice start to talk while they looked carefully around. Even the guard watched the speaker closely.

"On the count of three, run," said Granny Mac. "One, two, three."

With that, Bernie took off. It was a long way to the door, but the hope of seeing his parents, of somehow rescuing them, lent speed he didn't know he had.

The two steps leading up to the door had decorations like the steps out on the mountain. When Bernie reached them, he didn't hesitate, but started to scale the first by gripping the whorled designs with his fingers and toes.

He made it up the first step and checked behind him. None of the giants were looking, and both Tish and Granny Mac were almost at the steps.

Turning again, he was almost at the top of the second step when a brilliant flash lit up the cavern. The flash startled him so much he fell back onto the step.

A vast rushing, flapping sound came from overhead, and Bernie stared as a burst of flame shot forth in the air. It illuminated the space with a brilliance that hurt his eyes.

Dragons. There were three dragons swooping about and breathing fire. Their sleek dark bodies reminded Bernie of weasels, fierce and small but with wings like insects. The dragons dove upon the town, fierce claws extended and flames shooting out in quick, terrifying bursts. The giants scrambled for cover.

Desperate not to be stepped on by the giants or burned by the dragons, Bernie climbed the second step as fast as he could and threw himself into the opening. The dragons swooped by once more, making a cackling, squawking sort of noise, and then flew away up to the top of the cavern and out of sight.

Breathless, Bernie stared after them. The giants were standing up and dusting themselves off, when Bernie heard a voice say, "Merz, there's one a' yo' trolls loose."

He watched in horror as a huge hand swooped down and scooped up a wriggling, fighting Tish. "Oh no," he said, when he saw another troll run out and slash at the hand with a knife.

"There's another, and it's a fighter," the voice said, and another hand scooped up Granny Mac.

Bernie didn't have time to stare. He dashed through the opening and ran under the first piece of furniture he could make out, a sofa with barely enough space to squeeze under. It was low and dirty, but he was safe from view. Safe, but on his own in the stronghold of the giants.

TWO TOO MANY

PEERING OUT FROM UNDER THE EDGE OF THE CABINET, BERNIE heard muffled talking outside the door, but could make out only a few words, *banquet* and *five* and *dragons*. He still couldn't believe there were dragons. His dad had said dragons weren't real, but Bernie had seen them with his own eyes.

His dad. Bernie suddenly remembered his parents might be in the room, and he turned around to see what he could, glancing back now and then to watch for giants coming in the door.

The room was enormous, with heavy brown and gold rugs hanging on the walls. The patterns reminded Bernie of those on the steps outside on the mountainside. Around the room, there were windows, although it was lighter inside than out, so the windows were no more than empty black squares.

Below each window hung a torch, perhaps so the smoke could waft outside. Between the windows high up were shelves, and several of these held cages. Bernie saw flashes of movement from a couple of the cages, but couldn't see inside them with the light shining from below.

It didn't matter. At the sight of those cages, his heart leaped. He was sure his parents were up there. They had to be.

69

"How did you two get out? I told Verot those cages weren't sturdy, but I'd have thought they'd hold a couple of trolls."

Bernie guessed this was the giant the other had called Merz. He watched closely, and caught a glimpse of Tish, terror clear on her face. He had a sudden urge to leap out and wave to her, but his only chance to rescue her was to stay hidden. Still, he couldn't bear to see the look on her face.

"There, there, little one," said Merz, lifting Tish higher and higher into the air until she was at his eye level. "I wouldn't hurt you, but we've got no choice, don't you see."

Merz shook his head, and even from far, far below, his face looked sad.

"Now, let's put you back in your cage where you can rest comfortably. I'll fix it so you won't get out again, and I'll have Verot bring tidbits from the kitchen. Doesn't that sound nice?"

As he spoke, Merz reached up and lifted down a cage almost directly opposite from Bernie's hiding place.

"Strange, it's still locked." Merz held the cage up closer so he could look in. "Wait a minute, what's this?" He started counting out loud, "One two" and then looked into a cage still up on the shelf "and three four five." He shook his head, and then he looked back at Tish in one hand and Granny Mac in the other. "Where did you two come from? All the trolls we caught are still here, and you two look different. You've got hair, and you aren't green. What kind of trolls are you? You look like the Huldrefolk, though that isn't likely."

Bernie wondered why the giant sounded worried, but kept listening in case he heard anything that might help him rescue Tish and Granny Mac.

The giant, Merz, stood still for a minute, and then put the cage down on a table. He put Granny Mac and Tish down on the table as well. "Well, doesn't much matter what you look like, I'm afraid. You stay there while I open it up."

Tish ran over to where Granny Mac still lay, which was out of sight for Bernie. He hoped Granny Mac wasn't hurt but focused on the cage.

Inside, Bernie saw movement, and then his dad stood up and started talking to the giant, Merz. It was too far away for Bernie to hear more than a murmur, but he guessed the giant was getting a talking-to. Bernie caught a whiff of pepper in the air. Boy, his father must be angry.

Then, from an inside part of the cage, Bernie's mum appeared. She hurried over and talked to Bernie's dad, clearly trying to calm him down.

Bernie could barely breathe with excitement. If he was honest with himself, he had started to wonder if his parents could possibly still be alive, and there they both were. He wanted to run out and let the giant catch him, because then he and his mum and dad and Tish and Granny Mac would all be together. He would let his dad and mum take care of everything once again. They'd know what to do.

Bernie slid along the floor out into the room and stood up. He was too young to rescue anyone, too small to fight giants, and too scared to stay by himself any longer. As he straightened up, he saw his mum and nearly called out to her when a blow knocked him down. A huge foot rested against his side, in between him and the sofa under which he'd been hiding. Bernie heard a rumbling voice, "Merz, we got work to do. You got to stop messin' with those things. Leave 'em be. You don't need to be feeding them. They'll be gone soon enough, and it'll only be harder for ya if ya get stuck on 'em."

"Hush, now," Bernie could hear Merz say, "They can hear you. Don't need to frighten them, do you?"

"Bah, you're a softie, ya are," the other giant said. His foot started to rise into the air, and Bernie seized the chance to scoot back under the sofa. His eyes filled with tears, and he held his head in his hands. His dad and mum were locked in a cage, and from what the giant had said, something terrible would happen to them soon.

No, they depended on him. Bernie was going to have to find a way to rescue them. He wished he had any idea how. This wasn't a story, this was real life, and the hero was frightened, unprepared, and all alone.

16

UP THE DOWN TAPESTRY

BERNIE LAY ON THE FLOOR, OUT OF SIGHT OF THE GIANTS, BUT ABLE to see the cage with his parents by craning his neck. He came up with plan after plan for rescuing them but discarded each as unworkable.

There was no way around the fact his parents were locked up in a sturdy cage. Even if he could find a way to free them, they would have to escape past giants ten times his size.

Bernie wished he could talk to his parents, Tish, and Granny Mac. Together they might come up with a plan. He watched Merz close the cage on the table. It appeared Granny Mac was standing, though Bernie couldn't tell if Tish was holding her up or not.

Perhaps if he could climb one of the rugs, Bernie could get onto the table. The rugs hung almost all the way to the floor. He decided to try it as soon as the giant left.

His hopes were dashed a moment later when the giant lifted the cage and placed it back on the high shelf. Then, in a voice which carried down to where Bernie lay, he said, "I'm sorry, trolls. I wish we didn't have to... I wish it could be different."

The giant sighed loudly, patted the cage on the top, and then walked out the door.

Bernie wondered what Merz meant, but didn't dare stop to think about it. All the giants were outside, and he might not have such an opportunity again. The table top was much closer to the shelf, so he needed to get up there so he could shout to the cage. But first, he needed to cross the wide floor without getting caught.

The patterned floor had grooves deep enough Bernie worried he might twist an ankle or trip and fall if he stepped in one. He ran quickly, watching his feet and jumping over the grooves. Once or twice, he glanced out the door, biting his lip when he saw two giant men talking quite close to the entrance. They faced away, so they didn't see him, but it gave Bernie a scare.

Under the edge of the table, he hid behind one leg and caught his breath. He felt a little safer, although somebody might still see him if they glanced down.

Bernie studied the table. The legs were smooth and rounded, and he couldn't imagine climbing them. Maybe Tish could have, but not Bernie. At the far end of the table though, the leg stood close up against an embroidered rug displaying images of a giant fighting a huge boar, broadsword against ragged tusks.

The rug hung out of Bernie's reach except for tassels at the corners. He could reach those with only a small jump, and so by gathering his strength, he managed to get a good grip.

Trolls are strong by nature, but they are also heavy, and they almost never climb. Bernie pulled himself up, bit by bit, hoping his arms would hold out. About halfway to the top, the table leg bent in his direction, and that made it easier, as he could grip the wood between his legs and take some weight off his arms. Just then he sneezed. He wondered how long the rug had hung there. Dust floated in the air and tickled his nose. He sniffed and rubbed his nose against his shoulder.

Finally, he got his arms over the top of the table. It was

smooth, and he couldn't get much grip, but by clinging to the rug with his toes and edging himself forward, he made it onto the tabletop.

Panting, Bernie rolled over onto his back and studied the shelf. It was not as close as he had hoped. Besides, now that he was up on the table and out in the open, he risked being caught. Any giant walking into the room might see him.

Though he hated the idea, he wondered if he could climb the rug up to its top. It was a long way, and there was no table leg to help him. Even worse, the rug did not go close to the shelf the way it did to the table.

Growing desperate, Bernie looked at the wall, hoping to find something else he could climb. He noticed the rug was attached to the wall with iron rings, hidden from view by the tassels.

Curious, Bernie walked to the edge to see if there might be more rings to climb. There was one he might be able to reach, if he climbed onto the tassel and then swung around.

"I'll be fetching 'em, and taking 'em to the fire. There be no call for dragging food into the Council Chamber." The booming voice in the doorway made Bernie stagger back, and he had to grasp onto a tassel to keep from plunging to the floor.

A blond-haired giant with protruding ears stood outside the door, calling back over his shoulder. In moments, he'd be in the room. Bernie searched for someplace to hide, but the flat tabletop offered nothing to shield him.

As the giant ducked into the room, Bernie took a running leap for the ring behind the rug. His right hand closed on air, but his left managed to grab hold of the ring, and he clung to it for all he was worth. He dangled there, far above the hard, wooden floor, and tried to get his right hand up to the ring without banging into the rug.

If the giant saw the rug move, he'd be sure to investigate. Once, twice, three times, Bernie reached for the ring before he got his right hand on it and hung on for dear life.

"Why feed 'em, I says," the blond giant muttered to himself. "Only three days, for sure they can las' that long. Just a nuisance. But, Merz says feed 'em, so I gotta feed 'em."

On and on he went, recounting his miseries. Bernie paid little attention, but watched with a growing hope as the giant lifted all three cages down from the shelf to the table one by one. In the first, he saw two horses and some pigs. The second held a bear, growling and pounding on the wooden slats imprisoning him.

The last cage had barely crashed down on the table when the giant lifted them all together in his widespread arms and carried them away. In that instant, Bernie saw Tish clinging to the inside, and their eyes locked for the briefest moment before she was whisked away.

17

A DEADLY DROP

BERNIE CLUNG TO THE IRON RING, DESPAIRING. HIS ARMS ACHED, and he could barely hold on, much less leap back toward the table from where he hung. The floor lay far beneath him, and he didn't dare think what would happen if he fell.

His only hope was to pull himself up so he could rest on the iron ring while he figured a way down. Muscles burning, he inched up until the top of his head was barely through the ring. Swinging so momentum took the weight off his arm, he thrust it up through the ring and got his elbow hooked over one side.

Getting his other arm up was harder, but once he got it hooked as well, he pulled himself into a sitting position. The inside of the ring was embedded in the wall, so he had to sit precariously balanced with his back to the air, but at least he could rest.

Time passed, although in the dusky dim behind the rug, he had no sense of how long it might be. He searched for some way to grip the rug and climb down, but it was backed with a smooth material that offered nothing to grab onto.

In desperation, he tried to tear through the material to make his own handholds, but it was much too thick and strong for his bare hands. His despair and exhaustion deepened, and he had almost decided to leap to the floor and hope for the best when he heard a loud cough and shuffling footsteps in the room.

Perhaps he should shout out, and let the giant capture him. At least he would be safe for a while, and with his parents. While Bernie thought about this, he listened to the sounds the giant made. Something sounded odd, but Bernie didn't know what it could be.

Then the giant started to sing, or at least mumble, the words to a song:

When giants come stomping and knocking down trees
    Everybody scatters and hides.
    What could we be there for? Visiting? Please!
    We want what is tasty inside.

A feast's in the planning, but we need hors d'oeuvres
    Watch out if you're juicy and plump.
    A horse might go well with some piglet preserves
    Or a ram with an extra-large rump.

But most prized of all for our holiday feast
    (The thought of it fills me with glee)
    Lies deep down below, a magnificent beast,
    The Kraken, the king of the sea.

Below treacherous cliffs in the darkest fjords,
    we giants will search every inch
    Till we find younger kraken washed up on the shores
    Then we'll eat them with salt (just a pinch).

Bernie shuddered as the song trailed off, though if it were anything like troll songs, there were many more verses left unsung. He thought he recognized the voice as Merz, the giant who had captured Tish and Granny Mac, but his words were slurred and hard to understand.

From the room, there came a tremendous scraping noise. Then, without warning, the rug crashed back into the wall, and Bernie was thrown off his perch on the iron ring by a violent gust of air.

Scratching and grabbing, Bernie tried to catch hold of the rug, but there was nothing but smooth backing. He closed his eyes and prepared to die.

However, as he fell, the distance between the rug and wall grew smaller, until Bernie was scraping both. Then, with a whoomph, Bernie found himself laid out in a pinched area where the rug pressed against the wall. Whatever had thrust the rug against the wall had broken his fall, and while it would still be a jump to the floor, he could make it.

Looking down, he could see the legs of a chair, which the giant must have dragged over and pushed against the rug. Bernie could hear the giant's breath rumble through the rug, so he figured the giant must now be sitting in the chair and leaning back against the wall.

Bernie waited until the rumbling got more rhythmic, punctuated only by an occasional cough. Once he decided the giant was asleep, he edged over beyond where the rug was. He reached for a tassel, but as he grasped it, he slipped.

The landing jarred him, but he was unhurt. The giant still sat slumped against the wall. Murmuring a silent thanks to the deep-sleeping giant, Bernie got to his feet and hurried toward the door.

He didn't make it more than ten steps before a huge hand scooped him up.

"Well, look at what we have here," Merz said, scratching his neck with one hand while he held the other up to his eyes.

Bernie stood up unsteadily in the moving hand and looked at the giant face. He focused on Merz's eyes, while being careful not to look at the mouth with its enormous row of teeth.

"I am Bernie," he said with all the confidence he could muster. "You took my parents and my friends. I have come to rescue them." He wasn't sure why he said that, but it was the first thing which came out of his mouth.

Merz gaped at him and then laughed. Then the laugh turned into a cough, followed by an enormous sneeze, which knocked Bernie down. He clung to the giant's thumb so he wouldn't fall to the floor. He stood again, but kept a hand on the thumb to steady himself.

The giant rubbed his nose on his other sleeve. "Sorry, I've got a cold. You're a feisty one, aren't you? You've got nerve, I'll give you that." Peering closely, the giant asked, "How old are you, boy?"

"I am ten, sir," answered Bernie, figuring it would be wise to be polite to the huge man.

To his surprise, a huge teardrop and then another welled up in the giant's eyes, rolled down his face and onto his shirt, leaving dark patches. "The same age as my Fadz," he said, with sorrow in his voice.

"Is Fadz your son?" asked Bernie, not sure what to say, but curious at the words.

"Aye, he was."

Tears streamed down the giant's face, and Bernie felt a sudden wave of sympathy. "What happened?"

With a sudden snarl, Merz replied, "The dragons took him." He clenched his fist, and for a moment Bernie could not breathe as the fingers closed around him, but then Merz saw him struggling and relaxed his grip.

Leaning over, Merz placed Bernie on the tabletop. He scooted closer, the legs of the chair screeching as they dragged along the floor, and began to tell his story.

18

THE ENEMY OF MY ENEMY

"THE DRAGONS OF KING DARANEE ARE THE CAUSE OF ALL OUR problems," Merz started in a low conspiratorial whisper. Bernie almost gagged at the heavy smell of sour onions on Merz's breath but tried not to show it. "They want us to leave the mountain, but we have no place to go. Our people have lived under this mountain since before time began."

Bernie assumed that meant before anybody could remember, but the carved steps did look ancient. He nodded, hoping he looked sympathetic, although he was more worried about his parents than whatever troubled the giants.

Merz coughed hard, and the gust of stinky air almost knocked Bernie backward. "The mountain used to be full of light during the day, but the dragons locked the portals. They thought the endless night would drive us away. When we wouldn't leave, they insisted we do more and more for them and threatened to punish us for not obeying quickly. Though we try to satisfy them, it is almost impossible." A look of pain crossed his face, and there was a quaver in his voice when he went on. "Last year, we stood our ground and said we were done trying to meet King Daranee's endless demands.

"At first, they left us alone, and we celebrated and congratulated ourselves on standing up to the dragons. But a few days later, they flew in amongst our houses, burning anything left outside.

"Fadz was playing with a friend nearby. When the dragons came, the two ran for our house but never made it to the doorway."

"What happened to them?" asked Bernie, caught up now in the dreadful story.

"The dragons lifted them far into the air and dropped them down a chasm beyond the town. They fell to their deaths."

Bernie was horrified. "How could they? I don't understand. You are giants. Surely, you could fight the dragons and beat them." He thought about the three dragons in the public area outside. They were large, but not as large as the giants were. "You're bigger than they are."

Merz lowered his eyes. "If they didn't have fire, we could. In my great-grandfather's time, the dragons tried to rule Jötunheimr, but we giants fought them, throwing boulders and beating back the dragons with swords. For many years after that, the dragons and giants kept to themselves, but then when I was a child, the dragons learned to breathe fire. After that, we could not stop them."

"But, don't all dragons breathe fire?" asked Bernie in surprise.

"No," Merz said. "There is something they need to make the fire in their bellies, but we don't know what it is. We think it may be something they eat, something hidden from us. We have tried to learn their secret but have never succeeded."

"Why not?"

"Because we cannot fit into the caves the dragons have made high in the cavern. A few of our bravest giants climbed up to search for the secret, but the dragons breathed terrible fire on them, and they fell to their deaths. The dragon fire sticks to your flesh and burns until you are consumed."

For a few minutes, there was silence as Merz stared off into space. Bernie shuddered. His mind whirled as he tried to understand how the immense and awesome giants could be held hostage to anyone.

Then something occurred to Bernie. "Do the dragons have anything to do with why you kidnapped my parents and the other trolls?"

Merz looked ashamed but answered immediately. "Yes. The dragons want to have a banquet to celebrate the sixteenth birthday of King Daranee's only daughter, Mionaa. She, uh, developed a taste for trolls when she caught one near the mountains."

Bernie gasped. *A taste for trolls!*

"King Daranee demanded we provide the trolls and other delicacies for Princess Mionaa's sixteenth birthday. Dragons will not fly far from the mountains. They fear humans and their weapons.

"We said we would get horses and deer and pigs but not trolls. It is against our ancient customs to harm any creature with speech, except when we are attacked first, of course.

"But they threatened to come back and capture more of our children, to send fire into our houses and burn us out." Merz stopped. Anger crossed his face, but sadness as well. "We didn't have a choice. Even now, we don't know if we have enough trolls to satisfy King Daranee."

Bernie didn't know whether to be furious, understanding, or scared. While he felt sympathy for the giants, he couldn't let the dragons eat his mum and dad and Tish and Granny Mac. He wanted to argue, to plead, but instead he said something that surprised them both, "If I could find the secret of the dragon's fire, you might be able to stop them. If I did, would you let us go free?"

Merz started to laugh, then stopped and looked down at Bernie with a thoughtful expression. "You would be small enough to crawl into the dragon's den," he said, "but wouldn't you be afraid?"

"Of course I would," answered Bernie. "I'm already shaking so hard I feel like I'll break into pieces. But what choice do I have? The dragons will be here to eat my parents, my best friend, and probably me, if I don't go. If I succeed, I give us a chance, at least. You'd get a chance to fight back, too."

Merz sat, biting the end of his thumb. He sneezed again, turning away to keep Bernie from blowing off the table. Finally, he nodded. "Let's do it," he said. "There is a long ledge on the cliffs which reaches around close to the entrance of the cave. I'll get you that far. After that, it is up to you."

"How will I let you know if I figure out the secret or some other way to defeat the dragons?" asked Bernie, suddenly thinking of how dangerous it would be to walk back through town alone, even if he could get off the ledge. His knees shook and his heart pounded, but he tried not to let the giant see. Merz might be willing to help, especially when sick and missing his son. Any other giant would be a different story, and Bernie didn't want to be squashed if by some miracle, he did make it out alive from the dragons' caves.

Merz sat still, scratching his chin. Then, his eyes lit up. "There's a bench that used to be part of the guard post, back before the dragons breathed fire. It's close to the lair of King Daranee. I can leave you there, and then I'll go back once every two hours and wait for a signal."

He gave Bernie a long, pensive look, and Bernie worried he had changed his mind until he spoke.

"You're only ten, but you are extremely brave. I think my Fadz would have liked you." Merz said no more, but scooped Bernie up in one hand, walked across the hall and out the door.

Merz seemed a little unsteady on his feet. Bernie clung to the giant's fingers, wondering how sick the giant might be and trying not to think of the great height below him while they swayed their way past the edge of town and out into the dark. By the time they reached the abandoned guard post, Bernie's stomach hurt, and he was close to throwing up.

Away from the torches of town, a dim glow came from somewhere too low down for Bernie to see. There were also occasional flickers visible from the openings in the wall opposite from where they stood. Bernie guessed those must be where the dragons lived, and he shivered at the idea of the horrible dragon fire. He wanted to call out to Merz that he'd changed his mind, that there had to be a different way, but his throat closed up so he couldn't even squeak.

Reaching high over his head, Merz put Bernie down on the ledge he'd described. The giant pointed down to the left into the murky dark. "You can find the entrance down there. King Daranee lives in these caves, so they're guarded, but if you can find the secret anywhere, it will be there. I must leave before the dragon patrol gets back. Don't stay out here in the open too long."

Merz shifted uneasily back and forth on his feet. He pointed back where they had come. "I will be back there once every two hours. If you find something out, come to this ledge, and I'll watch for you." He suppressed a cough. "I've got to go so they don't hear me," he said, covering his mouth.

Bernie squinted where Merz had pointed and could barely make out a bench in the gloom far back from the cliff. It looked like the one outside the mountain. Bernie wished he were out there in the fresh air, far away from giants and dragons and the bitter taste of danger, which hung in the air. He wondered if it would be possible for the giant to see him from such a distance but decided he would deal with that problem if he ever got past the dragons, which seemed more and more unlikely.

Bernie choked out agreement. He looked at the narrow ledge disappearing off into the dark, leading to a cave he couldn't begin to imagine. What had he gotten himself into?

"Good luck," said Merz, before stifling a sneeze and hurrying back toward town.

Bernie suddenly wondered if the giant was too fuzzyheaded from his cold to even remember their plan or if he'd be too sick to come back. Putting the worries aside, Bernie turned and walked along the ledge toward the unseen cave. Whatever he was going to do, he needed to do it soon, while there was still time.

19

THE DRAGONS' LAIR

THE LEDGE WAS TREACHEROUS, CRUMBLING IN SOME PLACES AND fallen away entirely in others. Bernie crept along, feeling his way with his toes and hugging the cliff to make it past the gaps. Finally, he stumbled onto a wider bit of ledge and paused for a breath. He was startled to see the entrance near him, barely more than a large dark emptiness in the side of the cliff. He hesitated. The air reeked with a smoky stench like a camp fire doused in haste, but under the smoke hung an ominous scent of suspicion and watchfulness. Bernie braced himself and crept in the entrance, then waited while his eyes adjusted to the even dimmer light inside.

The cave quickly narrowed as he walked deeper in. The edges were jagged and uneven, and he wondered if the dragons folded their wings to get through the smaller parts of the passage. He walked on, and after a bit the cave grew wider, and the light grew brighter.

At first, Bernie couldn't tell where the light came from, as there were no torches, and the dim light seemed to come from all around him. When he looked closely at the walls, he could see a moss growing there, glowing with a faint luminescence. It didn't illuminate the space so much as give a sense of where the sides were. Bernie tried to pull a little moss off the wall, thinking it might be handy if he came to a place with no light at all, but it was tough and didn't budge.

He walked on. For a long time, the slap of his feet against the stone and the occasional clatter of loose rocks were the only sounds. Then, as he got deeper, he started to hear distant rumbles and murmurs, like a stream rushing down a hillside carrying pebbles and branches in its wake.

He walked more cautiously, staying in whatever shadows he could find, but he barely had time to duck when a dragon flew through the cave, rocketing over his head. Casting himself down, Bernie cowered as he waited for the dragon to turn back, to capture or perhaps eat him. He wished he had Tish's talent for staying hidden. For that matter, he wished he had Tish with him. She'd be brave. She'd know how to do this.

The dragon flew on. Bernie sat still, gasping. He needed to find a place to hide in case another, more attentive, dragon came along. He trotted along the rough wall, looking for a rocky over-hang or boulder to shield him from view.

He didn't find the hole so much as fell into it. With the lumi-nescent moss growing both inside and out, the hole blended with the walls.

Stooping down, Bernie peered around the hole. The air smelled better, not fresh but without the bitter taste of danger, which clogged the main passage. He rested just inside for a while, but as he did, he grew more and more curious about the hole. It seemed to be a tunnel, which curved out of sight. Tunnels must go somewhere. He wondered where.

There was room to crawl into the tunnel and enough space to turn around if it came to a dead end. Bernie chewed on his lip, trying to decide whether to explore the passage, when a flapping sound in the cave caused him to dive farther inside. He scurried around the bend. A moment later, he heard two separate swooshes from outside. From the sound of it, a pair of dragons had flown by.

Shivering, Bernie turned away from the main cave and continued down into the hole. As he crawled onward, he examined the strange round tunnel by the faint light from the moss. He wondered if it was natural or how it was made if it wasn't.

After a while, Bernie had lost track of time and had no sense whether he was anywhere near the main cave. He considered going back but had no better way of getting past the dragons than before. He couldn't figure out where the tunnel might be going but felt drawn forward by curiosity. Could a dragon even fit in here? If not, who made it, and why?

After a time, Bernie stopped. He knew he had to keep moving, but he'd been awake for many hours and been through so much his eyes refused to stay open. Trolls nap often, but there hadn't been a chance for days and days. Bernie lay down, and the silence in the tunnel enveloped him in a warm embrace. Resting his head on his folded arms, he closed his eyes and slept.

He woke with a start. There were voices, harsh screeching voices, and they sounded close. He twisted his head around but couldn't tell whether the voices were in front of him or behind. Probably behind. He sniffed, and a faint peppery smell tickled his throat. It smelled like anger.

Scrambling to his hands and knees, he hurried forward, listening as he went. The slapping of his palms on the tunnel floor sounded abnormally loud, and he slowed to minimize the noise. The voices had stopped, and he waited to see if he had gotten away from them or if they might be listening for him.

Bernie's head bumped the ceiling. The tunnel was smaller here. Where before he could sit up or crawl without touching, now he had to crouch low to keep from scraping his head.

He eased himself forward. Trolls are comfortable underground, but he still sensed the enormous weight of the mountain above him.

I'm going to die in here, trapped in a hole.

He shook off the feeling. Somewhere in here was the secret to the dragon's fire. Somehow, he had to find it. Now, Bernie hoped the voices had been in front of him. Maybe if he could hear them, he'd discover something about their secrets. He listened again but the passage was silent.

Suddenly, beyond a corner, Bernie came to the end of the tunnel. In front of him was a wall.

Trapped. The tunnel had gotten narrower as he crawled and was too small to turn around in. Bernie didn't know how far he would have to crawl backward before he could turn. Even if he did, where would he go?

Reaching ahead, Bernie put his hand on the wall. The texture was different than the tunnel, and he felt a grain running through it. It was made of wood, not stone. He pushed against the barrier, but it didn't budge. Pressing his nose up against the surface, Bernie sniffed. The peppery smell lingered, but stronger was the smell of smoke. The smoke was fresh, like that from a fire his mum would make in the winter. A tear rolled down Bernie's cheek, but he brushed it away. No time.

Perhaps it was a door, which might mean a catch somewhere around. He felt around the edge where the wooden part met the stone, but he could feel nothing.

Frustrated, Bernie scratched at the door again. He felt it give a bit, not outward but sideways. Prying his fingernails into the tiny gap he had made on one side, he pushed hard, and the edge moved a bit further.

About to shove it once more, Bernie smelled a stronger whiff of smoke and caught a glimpse of light on the other side of the wooden barrier. It was not the faint glow of the moss but a flickering light.

It was a fire. Pushing close to the small opening, Bernie peered through. On the other side, he could see a small, but blazing, fire in a pit. The crackle of the burning logs suggested they had been added quite recently.

Bernie peered around the cave within, although he could not see much. He started to shift the barrier a bit further when a high-pitched voice sounded, close enough to startle him. He stopped and listened to what sounded like a whiny female dragon.

"I don't care about the stupid banquet. Hurrah for you; you bossed around a bunch of dumb giants. I want to go places and see the world. I want to catch my own trolls, burn my own villages. You never let me go anywhere."

A deeper voice spoke in a tone which froze Bernie's blood. How could anyone talk back to the owner of that voice?

"You know you can't leave the mountain. I won't hear any more about it. Do you understand?"

"But, Daddy, why not? All the stories talk of adventures out in the world, of gobbling up brave knights and killing innocent maidens." The younger dragon sounded wistful, but Bernie shook at the sound of those terrible deeds.

"Stories. Enough with the stories. We rule the mountain, and the giants bow down to us and pay us tribute. That was honor enough for my father, and it is enough for me as well."

The male dragon's tone made it clear his decision was final, but she persisted. "But, Daddy, I want to go out in the daylight."

"Enough!" he roared. "Mionaa, you will be at the banquet tomorrow, and you will cease all talk of leaving the mountain, or I will forbid you going out, even at night."

His voice lowered, and he went on solemnly, "Dragons never go out in the daytime while Tagatzur prowls the hills. We must not face him."

Even the whiny child seemed to understand she had gone too far. "Yes, Father," she said.

There was a loud clatter, and Bernie saw a large, fierce dragon sweep out of the cave. He had called her Mionaa, the name of the princess Merz had mentioned, so that must be King Daranee. But who was this *Tagatzur*, and why did he scare the dragons? Bernie shivered at the idea of yet another danger, but knew he had to go on, so he squared his shoulders and turned back toward the crack of light.

2 0

A PETULANT PRINCESS

BERNIE WATCHED THROUGH THE CRACK FOR A CHANCE TO GET OUT to explore the cave. While he was crawling down the tunnel, he'd thought about the dragon's secret. Merz had said it might be something they ate or drank. Unfortunately, Bernie had no idea what they normally ate. He didn't even want to think about it with his mum, dad, and Tish and Granny Mac all locked in a cage, waiting for the banquet.

Could it be that eating trolls was the secret? It didn't seem likely. Nothing about trolls would light on fire, except a small bit of gas when they'd eaten too many newts.

No, whatever it was, the dragons must keep it close by. Maybe something that bubbled up from deep beneath the earth.

Bernie stopped. Maybe it grew outside. Bernie thought suddenly of the shadow that swooped over him on Mount Dreadful while the other two trolls slept. It must have been a dragon. King Daranee had said something about going out at night. Perhaps whatever it was could only be found outside.

Bernie sat, dejected. He had no way to get out of the mountain, no way to search for whatever the secret might be. He wasn't going to be able to save the trolls or even himself.

94

Suddenly, Bernie turned back to the barrier. While he'd been thinking, the sounds of movement on the other side had stopped. He peered this way and that but could see nothing. He would have to risk being heard. He pushed and managed to move the wood a little farther out of the way.

Reaching into the gap with his fingers, he tugged and pulled. Slowly, in fits and starts, it shifted until he could stick he head through to look around.

The cave beyond was not large but did go back quite far. Fire-light illuminated the whole cave, and Bernie looked carefully to be sure there wasn't a dragon lurking in some corner.

When he was convinced it was empty, he slid the wood further until he could climb out. As he could not turn around, he had to drop down headfirst and roll when he hit the floor.

Rubbing his head, he stood up and looked back around. Beyond the fire, he could see the passage out into a larger cavern. If he couldn't find any answers here, he'd have to explore out there next.

Before searching the cave, Bernie wrestled the wooden barrier back into place. From this side, he could see the barrier was a wooden case holding oddly shaped rocks, some long and skinny, others round, many with jagged edges.

Bernie stared at them. He couldn't understand what they were or why they were there. Then he laughed, though he quickly clapped his hands over his mouth. He couldn't afford to make a noise.

It was a rock collection, like Tish's collection of pretty stones. This must be Mionaa's private cave and her collection. For a moment, Bernie thought of Mionaa as a girl like Tish, but her terrible words came back to him, *gobbling up brave knights and killing innocent maidens.*

He must not forget Mionaa was a dragon. Because of her, his parents were kidnapped and might be eaten any time. He had to find a way to save them.

The passageway outside Mionaa's chamber was empty, but Bernie knew she or another dragon might come along at any time. So much bitter danger taste hung in the air he found it hard to breathe. Faint murmurs like distant voices echoed against the walls, but he couldn't tell where they came from. He couldn't see more than a few feet in each direction and had no idea where to start.

He wanted to go back through Princess Mionaa's cave and hide in the tunnel, but he knew he had to move forward. As he looked around, heart pounding in his chest, an odd bubble of something different broke through the bitter taste. He sniffed, trying to find it, and a few moments later, smelled another. The aroma seemed out of place in this dark, smoky chamber, and it took him a minute or two to recognize the bubbles as butterscotch. "Secrets," he whispered out loud.

Another bubble led him to the left. He shivered at the idea of intentionally walking toward dragons but crept on down the passage, following the occasional butterscotch bursts as they grew stronger. As he went, he stared at a series of intricate sculptures, which lined the passageway. They stood on pedestals of different sizes, but the shapes were wild and twisted, and he couldn't tell what they were meant to be.

Some of the sculptures were large enough to hide behind, and Bernie darted from one of these to the next. At any moment, he expected a dragon to stride down the passage and discover him, but none appeared.

Ahead of him, the passage took a sharp turn, and Bernie heard sounds beyond, so he tiptoed close and listened. The voice he had heard before, the king's voice, sounded muffled, but there were other voices. None seemed close, so Bernie peeked around the corner.

He jerked his head back at what he saw. A little beyond the curve, two dragons lay in the passage, one on each side of a grand entrance.

Guards. It must be the king's court. He was relieved neither guard saw his head, but he couldn't chance one looking his way again. Instead, he cupped his hands to his ears and listened, staying out of sight of the guards.

Another pop of butterscotch gave him courage. He could make out a few snatches of speech, especially when the voices were raised. Fortunately, the king's deep voice carried well.

"... don't like it, sire. ... to drive the giants from ... and for all." This voice was high and reedy.

"But how would ... gather such delectable morsels ... feasts?" the king responded. "If we ... Tagatzur ... steal our power."

"... restless. They ... ready ... rebellion. ... don't need trolls ..." the reedy voice continued. "... lost a soldier for months ... chased ..."

"Enough!" snapped the king, sounding every bit as annoyed as he had with the princess. "... another chance, but after that ..."

Bernie heard no more, as a clatter of claws and rush of wings made it clear the king was leaving the chamber. Realizing the dragons might head in his direction, he ran as fast as he could back toward Princess Mionaa's cave. Panting and huffing, he collapsed on the floor.

For a short while, Bernie heard nothing but his own ragged breath, and he calmed down. He started to think he might be able to sneak back out down the passage but stopped when he heard a commotion headed his way.

Bernie scrambled to his feet and ran toward the entrance to the small tunnel. There was no mistaking the voice, which grew louder by the moment. His only chance was the tunnel, but first he had to move the heavy shelves out of the way.

"You may not wear your mother's jewelry, young lady," the king's voice thundered from the passageway, peppery anger filling the air. Bernie put his back against the shelves holding the rock collection and shoved hard. It resisted and then jerked suddenly to reveal the entrance to the tunnel. A couple of the stones fell from the shelves to the ground, but Bernie had no time. He clambered up into the hole.

Pulling the wood back over the hole was out of the question, as Bernie couldn't turn around. Instead, he held still, trying not to make noise and hoping the opening would go unnoticed.

"How many times must I talk to you about this, Mionaa?" The king's voice rang loudly, and Bernie shook with fear. The king must be in Mionaa's chamber itself.

"Well, why not?" Mionaa whined, "It's not like she has any use for it."

"Mionaa, how dare you? Those are your mother's jewels."

"Daddy," Mionaa said in a softer voice, "she's dead."

There was a silence. Bernie could hear the dragons breathing and waited.

"I know, Mionaa, I know. I am sorry, but those are jewels for a queen, and you are still a young princess." His voice sounded heavy.

"I won't be forever, daddy," Mionaa said, but the argument was gone from her voice.

Bernie hoped they would leave soon. He needed to get back to Merz, and he couldn't move while they were so close. He waited, listening to the fire crackle and the dragons' raspy breath.

"Mionaa, why is your fire flickering? It's almost as if there is a draft."

Bernie heard the king moving about, but then Mionaa's voice, quite close to him. "It's nothing, father. What an imagination you have. Why look, some of my stones have fallen. I must have moved…"

There was a scraping sound, and the wood barrier was back in front of the hole. Bernie lay stunned for a moment. *She knew about the hole but didn't want her father to know. Why?*

It didn't matter; he should grab at his chance to escape. Scrabbling through the tunnel as quickly as he could, he headed for the outside cavern where he would wait for Merz.

AN UNKNOWN FOE

As he scrambled, Bernie repeated the message over in his head. *The dragons are afraid of Tagatzur, who only comes out in the daytime. Tagatzur steals their power.* He said it again and again, afraid of it slipping away.

What did it mean? It sounded important. Maybe Merz would know who Tagatzur was and could get him to help fight the dragons. With such valuable information, the giants would let his parents and Tish and Granny Mac go free.

The tunnel was bigger here, and Bernie could run crouched over. *Dragons afraid of Tagatzur, only comes out in daylight. Steals power.* He muttered it aloud, holding on to the precious information.

At last, ahead of him, he saw the outer passage. Close to escape, but he had to be careful. He poked his head out and looked to his left and to his right. No dragons.

Climbing out of the tunnel, he breathed a sigh of relief. He was going to make it. It was only a little way to the entrance of King Daranee's lair. From there, he would go to the other end of the ledge to wait for Merz.

"Going somewhere?" The high-pitched voice over his head

made his blood run cold. He looked up. Mionaa hung upside down, clutching the roof of the cave with her claws.

Bernie squeaked. It wasn't a brave, heroic squeak either, but a terrified, desperate troll-squeak.

Mionaa laughed and let go of the ceiling, flipping over expertly to land in front of him, blocking his way back into the tunnel. "A troll. I knew somebody was using my old tunnel, but how tasty to find a troll."

Bernie backed up until he ran into the wall.

Mionaa chuckled. "Now, I must decide whether to eat you raw or toast you first."

"You don't want to eat me," whimpered Bernie. "I, er, am too tough for such a, um, delicate princess dragon's stomach."

Mionaa's smile disappeared, and the rumble deep inside her sounded like an angry thunderstorm. "I am not *delicate*," she snarled at him, puffs of smoke shooting from her nostrils. "Don't call me that, you ugly toad." Sparks flew from her mouth as she talked, and Bernie scrambled to avoid being burnt.

Mionaa extended one especially sharp claw. She slowly waved it in front of him, and then without any warning, jabbed it into his right shoulder and pulled it out, all before he could react.

It took a moment before the pain hit Bernie, and by then, Mionaa had jabbed him again, first in his stomach and then in the right arm, right below his shoulder.

The pain was bad, but trolls are tough, so there was only a small amount of blood at each wound. The shoulder bled the most.

Mionaa cocked her head sideways and looked at him. "You are tough," she said, "so perhaps we should soften you up." She rubbed her claws together, and they made a sound like knives being sharpened.

"What… what are you going to do?" Bernie asked, squeezing his right shoulder to stop the bleeding.

"Me? I'm not going to do anything much," she said with a

wicked smile. She launched into the air, her talons clutching Bernie's arms, but not piercing them this time. Bernie screamed, but Mionaa ignored him and flew out the entrance of the cave and up into the air.

"You are the one who is going to do something," she said with the air whistling past.

As she slowed down, Bernie could see the lights of the giant's town, flickering far below and off to his left. Below, he could see nothing.

"What am I going to do?" Bernie asked through clenched teeth, although he had a good guess.

Mionaa chortled. "You are going to..." Mionaa let go, and Bernie felt the rush of air. Faintly, behind him, he heard her call out, "...fall."

Trolls are tougher than people, even tougher than giants for their size, but they are not tough enough to fall from a great height and land on rocks without harm. Such a fall would kill any troll, and Bernie was no exception.

As the air whistled by, Bernie thought with sorrow of his parents and Tish and Granny Mac, all about to be eaten by Mionaa and the dragons. He thought of the secret he would not have time to tell the giants.

However, when Bernie landed, it was not on rocks. It was on Merz, and the giant and the troll fell together with a mighty thump onto the ground. Bernie had the air knocked out of him, and Merz didn't look much better, but when they finally got back to their feet and brushed themselves off, neither had any serious injuries.

"What were you doing up there?" Merz asked. His voice wobbled a bit, and he appeared dazed by the impact.

"Mionaa dropped me," Bernie gasped, trying to gather his wits. There was something important he had to say, but it had been knocked clean out of him. Something about dragons. Something secret.

"Why did she drop you instead of eating you?" Merz asked.

To Bernie, it seemed a rude question, but he explained Mionaa wanted to soften him up *before* she ate him.

"Wait. That means..." Merz started, when there was a rush of wings and talons. Merz covered his face, and Bernie threw himself behind the giant's legs.

"*My* troll," screeched Mionaa, and she dove toward Bernie, swooping around Merz and barreling down on him.

"Leave him alone," roared Merz, batting at Mionaa and knocking her tumbling through the air.

She righted herself and flew straight at his head, but when he covered his face, Mionaa switched direction and latched onto Bernie's shoulders.

Desperate to free himself, Bernie whacked at the dragon and dislodged the talons from one shoulder. Dangling, he hit her again but then felt a tremendous yank on his legs.

Merz had grabbed him from below and pulled him back down. Mionaa was still hooked onto Bernie's shoulder, which felt like it was on fire. She tried to loosen herself, but Merz had grabbed her around the throat.

With one hand, Merz freed Bernie from the dragon's grip. With the other, he held her by the throat so she could not breathe fire and burn them.

When Bernie was free, Merz threw Mionaa into the air. She struggled upright and glared at him. "You will regret that, giant," she shouted down. "When my father hears you mistreated a dragon princess, he will unleash terror on your town such as you have never seen." Then, without waiting for a response, Mionaa whirled around and disappeared into the darkness.

Merz and Bernie stared after her. Then, Merz picked up Bernie and hurried toward the town. "We have to warn the guard. King Daranee will be furious, and if he attacks, we need to be ready."

Bernie's teeth chattered with the force of the giant's footsteps, but he shouted the fragments of the secret which were slowly coming back to him. "Dragons afraid of … daylight. Steals power."

"What did you say?" asked Merz, slowing to a walk. "What was that?"

HELP AT ANY SIZE

"Oh, I've got it all wrong," Bernie said miserably. "There is something missing. Something about a terrible creature, but I can't remember his name. The dragons are afraid of him."

"But what did you say?" Merz asked again, insistently. He stopped walking, and stared at Bernie.

"Dragons afraid of something-something daylight. Steals power," Bernie said again, "but that's wrong because…"

He stopped. "Wait a moment." He thought hard, so hard his ears lifted straight out.

"The dragons are afraid of daylight," he said softly, and then louder again for Merz. "The dragons are afraid of daylight!" It all made sense. King Daranee telling Mionaa she couldn't go out during the day. The voice in the chambers talking about the soldier lost for a year after chasing a giant. The rule of darkness the dragons imposed on the giants.

Merz chewed on his thumb, lost in contemplation. "But then, we have a way to fight back. We need to open the portals."

Not waiting to explain, Merz ran again, faster even then before. Bernie would not have been able to speak if he had tried. All he could manage was to keep himself from throwing up.

As they rushed into town, uniformed giants stood to bar his way, but he called to them, "Sound the horns; gather all able-bodied giants to the town center. The dragons are coming to attack."

The guards pulled horns from their belts and sounded them with an intricate set of calls. A great hue and cry went up from those in sight, and more giants poured out of their doors and ran toward the center.

For a while, it was bedlam, and Bernie clung to Merz's hand, afraid he would be trampled if he slipped down. When a crowd had gathered in the center, Merz made his way through and addressed them.

"This brave troll," Merz began, but then had a coughing fit and had to stop and hold Bernie high up for the crowd to see. Bernie felt quite sick and not the least brave, but there didn't seem to be any need to say anything.

"This brave troll," Merz began again, "has gone alone into the dragon's lair, and he brings us news."

At this, the crowd buzzed and chatted until Merz had to shout for quiet. He then held up Bernie, who spoke in his loudest, clearest voice, "My friends, I have news for you."

Unfortunately, nobody could hear him, so after a couple of attempts, Merz suggested Bernie let him tell the story. Bernie agreed, so Merz started talking and explained how Bernie had overheard the dragons and learned their secret weakness. He made Bernie sound far braver than he remembered being, but maybe Merz thought that would help convince the other giants.

Finally, Merz finished the tale. "And now, we must open the portals over the city before the dragons arrive. By the light of Tagatzur, we shall find our strength and their weakness."

Bernie's head popped up from where it had been drooping. He had not slept in a long, long time, but the name was familiar. "Merz," he asked, "Who is Tagatzur? He is the one the dragons were talking about."

"It's an old word from an ancient language. It is the name for the sun."

For a while, the giants bustled around, organizing who would go to the portals, but then a problem arose. An elderly giant with a stooped back and white hair told Merz the key to the portals had been taken and destroyed by King Eradenee, father of King Daranee.

"We will break the locks if we must," Merz said, but he looked worried.

"Please, could you free my parents?" Bernie begged Merz. "We could help."

Merz looked at Bernie and started to laugh. "How could you little trolls help us?" he said, waving to the giants thronged around the square. "I will let the trolls out," he said, "but I want you to stay here where you will be safe. We appreciate all you have done, but this is a job for the giants."

Without waiting for a response, Merz strode into the council chambers. He reached up and pulled down cage after cage, placing them on the floor. He opened the cage with Bernie's parents, and they rushed out and embraced him.

"Now, you trolls stay here where it's safe," he boomed. Then, softly, he said to Bernie, "I am leaving the key to the cages with you. If anything happens to us, let the animals go…" He put the key down and stood, gave them a quick nod and left to join the other giants.

After giving his mum and dad great troll hugs, Bernie noticed Tish standing behind them, looking shy. He ran over and took her hand. "Are you okay? How is Granny Mac?"

Before Tish could answer, Granny Mac hobbled up. She had a limp she hadn't before, but otherwise looked as well as ever. "Tish told me over and over you would come back for us."

Bernie looked at Tish, and she blushed and looked away. He kicked the ground and rubbed his neck. To break the silence, he told them about the dragons and how the giants were off to open the portals.

"Granny Mac, I think they need our help." Bernie felt foolish saying it, and he couldn't have asked his own mum and dad, but she might understand.

Granny Mac looked at him curiously for a moment, then nodded. "Do what you must, but take care of Tish, please."

Bernie nodded and gave her a quick hug. He turned to his parents and Tish, who all stood watching him as if he had sprouted wings. "Come on, we need to free the horses."

Bernie tried to pick up the key, but he could barely get it off the ground by himself. He felt a hand on his shoulder and looked back to see his father taking the other end.

They carried the key to a cage with two horses. Hefting it over their shoulders, they turned the key in the lock.

"Trolls don't ride horses," Bernie's father said to him.

"I'm going to try," Bernie answered. "It would take too long for us to walk." He stood, looking at the horse, which towered over him, and said, "Could you give me a hand getting up?"

Bernie's mum ran over and hugged him again, telling him to be careful, but then offering her back for him to climb on. His dad helped steady Bernie, who climbed up on his mum, then reached for the horse's mane.

With some help, he managed to clamber up, but then sat, not moving. A moment later, Tish climbed up on his mother's back and said, "You aren't going without me, are you?"

"Not this time," Bernie laughed and helped her up in front of him, where she stroked the horse's mane. "Do you know how to ride one of these?" he asked her.

"I've never been on one," admitted Tish, "but Granny has, and she says you need to talk nicely to it and it will take you where you want." Leaning forward, Tish patted the horse and said, "Please, will you help us follow the giants?"

The mare whinnied and started forward. "Hold on," cried Tish.

Bernie put his arms around her, and they both clung to the horse's mane. As the horse cantered forward, Bernie thought that after the ways he had traveled recently, hanging from a dragon's talons, carried in a giant's hand, this wasn't too bad. He was also glad to be with Tish again.

Even in the dark cavern, it was not hard to follow the giants. They were ahead, singing as they marched and carrying torches, which flickered like fireflies in the dark.

It was Tish who first saw the dragons. "Look," she cried, pointing into the dark ahead of them. The dragons themselves weren't visible until one breathed fire, which flashed in the dark like distant lightning. In the flash, the circling dragons could be seen, diving and attacking the giants.

"We've got to hurry," Bernie said and urged the horse forward. Its gentle canter turned into a brisk trot and finally a gallop.

The trolls hung on for dear life. Bernie would have preferred the giant, and perhaps even the dragon, to this headlong, rolling ride where the pounding feet threatened to shake them loose at any moment.

Up ahead, the sounds of fighting shattered the stillness of the cavern. Shouts and screeches and all manner of clashing weapons and claws filled the air.

Beyond the main fighting, there was a cluster of torches. Bernie could see Merz standing with two other giants. They took turns pounding on something.

"Go around the fighting. We need to help Merz," he called out to Tish over the battle noises.

"Who is Merz?" she asked.

"Never mind, just go that way," Bernie called, and Tish patted the galloping horse and talked until it ran to the left, into the darkness away from the battle.

"They need to open the portals," Bernie managed to get out

between the pounding thud of the horse's hooves. "They are locked, and I think you can help."

"Me?" said Tish, half turning and almost knocking them off the horse.

"Hang on, I'll tell you when we get there," said Bernie, breathlessly. He didn't know if he could hang on but was terrified of the sharp hooves below him.

They galloped on, until ahead of them they could see the three giants. It did not look like they were having any success with the huge, iron lock.

"Merz," called out Bernie at the top of his voice as the mare slowed and stopped near the giant's legs. When Merz didn't look, Bernie called again, and Tish joined in. Finally, Merz looked down and saw them.

"What are you doing here?" he asked, irritation in his voice. "I told you to wait in the chambers."

"This is my friend, Tish. I think she can help." Bernie spoke quickly.

Merz looked at Tish, sitting on the horse. She waved at him, and called up, "Nice to meet you."

"Tish is clever with her hands, and she's smaller than I am. I think she might be able to spring the lock."

"Well," said Merz doubtfully, "I guess we could…"

They didn't hear what he guessed because out of the air a rush of wings and talons bowled into Tish and Bernie, knocking them off the horse and down onto the ground.

23

THE ENEMY'S STRENGTH

WITH A SCREECH, THE DRAGON CIRCLED AROUND THE HORSE, grabbing for the trolls, but Bernie grabbed Tish and dragged her out of the way. "Come on," he shouted, running toward the giants who stood by the great lock.

Moments later, more screeches and cries announced the arrival of other dragons. Bernie didn't know how many there were, but he could see the giants flailing at them in the dark.

The dragons seemed to have learned to attack the torches first and soon had knocked out both, leaving the trolls and giants in deep darkness, broken only by flashes from the dragons as they attacked the giants. They would swoop down and breathe fire at the giants, who were soon dancing around to avoid the flame and waving clubs and swords into the dark.

One dragon was hit with a lucky swing, and it crashed into the ground. Not dead, but simply hurt, it breathed fire when the giants came close. It was by that light Bernie and Tish made it to the locks.

The giants had been using a wooden-handled sledge hammer to pound at the lock, and its head rested on the ground while the handle leaned against the lock.

"Climb the handle," panted Bernie, and Tish scrambled up onto the handle ahead of him. The handle was rough wood and easy to grip, and they started to climb up. It was slow going, but they had almost made it when pain seared across his back.

"Stay away from the lock," hissed the dragon, wheeling in the air and flying back toward Bernie.

"Keep climbing," Bernie called to Tish, fending off the talons with one arm but feeling himself slipping. He grabbed the wooden handle with both arms and clung to it, even when the dragon raked him again with its claws.

Just as Bernie thought he could not hold off the attack any longer, the dragon gave a high-pitched shriek and tumbled toward the ground. Merz stood beside Bernie and raised a huge boot over the dragon's crumpled form.

Bernie didn't wait. He climbed up after Tish, who stood on the edge of the keyhole, lit for a moment by another dragon's fire. "Inside," he called, and she turned and slipped inside the hole.

Bernie squeezed in after her, but the darkness inside was absolute. Bernie had no idea what the inside of a lock should look like or how to start trying to unlock it. To make matters worse, the floor was uneven and shifted when he tried to walk forward.

"What are we supposed to do?" Tish asked.

"I don't know," said Bernie. All his courage of the last hours seemed to drain away. Why had he thought they could help? He had put himself and Tish in terrible danger, and for what? "If only we could see, we might be able to work the lock," Bernie said.

He slumped down. Outside the battle raged, and it sounded as if both giants and dragons were closer. Shouts and crashes punctuated the darkness, but no light entered the lock.

Bernie felt around with his hands. There was something like interlocked teeth, but no matter how he pushed and pulled at them, nothing seemed to happen. Some moved, while other were frozen in place, but without light, he didn't know how to work the lock.

Tish stood and tried, but she had no better luck. "We need light," she said to Bernie. "Maybe you could get one of the torches the giants dropped."

"They're much too big," he said. "Besides, the dragons would never let me go out and get one."

Then an idea struck him. "Tish," he said, "get ready to work the locks, because it may get a little hot in here."

He stumbled through the dark to the key opening. Tish called out behind him, "What are you doing?" but Bernie didn't answer. He was afraid if he said it aloud, it would sound too foolish and he'd lose his nerve.

Leaning out the keyhole, Bernie saw flashing dragons and fighting giants, although many of the giants appeared to be hurt. He watched for a dragon to fly close, and when one did, he shouted, "Hey, you, cowardly dragon. I bet even Princess Mionaa could fight better than you."

The dragon whirled around, eyes blazing in the dark. He dove for Bernie, who threw himself back inside with a squeak. He hadn't expected his idea to work so well.

"What are you doing?" Tish shouted. "That dragon is going to…"

And the dragon did. A spout of flame roared through the keyhole, heating the air and illuminating the inside. Somebody, perhaps the dragons, had piled stones and dirt inside the lock, but most of it was near the keyhole "Quick," Bernie said, "start working on the lock." As he did so, he reached over and picked up a stone and threw it as hard as he could out the opening at the dragon.

Tish spun around. Some of the flames stuck to the sides of the lock, so it was no longer pitch black. She pressed down on some parts and up on others, but they kept falling back when she moved on. "These bottom teeth need to go down, and the top teeth need to go up," she said. "But they won't stay in place."

Bernie didn't answer, as he was busy throwing rocks at the dragon. Fire rushed into the opening again, and he barely got himself out of the way in time. "You can do it, Tish. I know you can," he called out to her. He hoped he was right. Picking up a particularly large stone, he stumbled toward the keyhole, thinking perhaps he could block the entrance somewhat.

"Wait, don't throw it," Tish said, urgency in her voice. "We need to make *langises*, and we'll need all of these."

Bernie looked back at her, confused for a moment, but then he saw Tish pile two rocks on one of the lock's teeth. It stayed down. He stared, then hurried to her side. Flames poured through the entrance again, and the lock rocked slightly as if a dragon or giant had collided with it, but Bernie and Tish ignored it and piled rocks on top of the teeth to hold them down.

The piles holding up the upper teeth were harder, but after a couple of piles collapsed and both trolls had sore feet, they got the first pile high enough. Bernie pushed harder on the upper tooth and Tish slipped a rock in to keep it in place. One more tooth and they'd have it.

Suddenly, a crashing sound at the entrance was followed by a large rock flying through the air. "Hurry," shouted Tish, as they piled rocks on each other as fast as they could. When they reached the top, and the final tooth was wedged in place, she pointed to a gear close behind the teeth. "We need to push that."

Another spout of flame lit up the lock, and then another. Bernie looked, and saw the iron was starting to glow red.

"He's trying to melt the lock so it can't open," he yelled to Tish.

"No need to shout," she said, working in the dim light from the glowing metal. "I can see it. Push on the gear!"

Bernie edged closer and pushed, but the gear wouldn't budge. Tish squeezed in beside him, and the two used their shoulders to shove as hard as they possibly could. At first, the gear held firm, but finally it shifted, making a great creaking noise when it did. As they kept shoving, the gear moved more quickly until suddenly it stopped, and would not move any further.

"Look!" Tish pointed up, and Bernie could see the sides of the lock were split, but even so, the gear was jammed.

"Give me a minute. I'm sure I can figure it out." Tish poked at the gear. "We're so close. We can't give up now."

Bernie stood for a moment and then laughed. "Tish," he said, "we are trolls!"

Tish didn't move for a moment, but then her face lit up. "Yes!" She reached down and grabbed one of the larger rocks and bashed it against the gear, breaking off chunks of the metal. Bernie grabbed a jagged rock, and they battered and rammed the shattered gear, laughing as they did, until finally it budged.

"Watch out!" Tish grabbed at the side of the lock, but the two sides had split farther apart. Tish screamed and toppled down toward the gap. Bernie let go of the rock he held and leapt toward her. The weight of his body threw her away from the opening, but landed them both against the hot metal.

Jerking back from the heat, Bernie pulled Tish away as well. The two backed up to the edge of the gap, but the heat was growing unbearable. "We'll have to climb out," said Bernie, turning around and feeling for anything they could step on.

The other side of the gear protruded outside the gap, so Bernie put one foot on it to test whether it was strong enough. It held, so he stood on it and bounced up and down. It still held.

"Climb down with me," he called to Tish, and she threw her legs over the side and climbed on to the gear, although it was difficult for them both to balance.

Their combined weight must have been too much, as the gear snapped loudly and disappeared out from under them. Tish managed to grasp the bottom edge of the lock, and Bernie grabbed her legs as he fell.

For a moment, they simply hung, when out of the dark came the dragon, shrieking and spitting. "Jump," yelled Bernie. He let go of Tish and leaped down on the dragon's wing. He felt the whole dragon shift as Tish landed on the other wing. "Hang on," he shouted, but Tish didn't need to be told. The wings were leathery with sharp ridges they could grab hold of.

The dragon was furious and wild. It tried to shake them off, but they clung to each wing, making it difficult for the dragon to fly. Bernie thought it would have to land, but the dragon showed its strength and determination by slowing lifting into the air, flapping its wings furiously to stay aloft.

24

BLINDED BY THE LIGHT

"WE HAVE TO LET GO," SCREAMED TISH AS THE GROUND SLIPPED away beneath them.

"It's too late," shouted Bernie. He looked around wildly for some way to escape, but all he saw was a giant, waving a club through the air. It was Merz, but the giant obviously didn't see the two trolls.

"Merz," screamed Bernie. "The portals are unlocked. Open the portals."

The giant hesitated. "Bernie?" he called out.

"We're on the dragon," Tish and Bernie shouted together. This time the giant heard. Jumping in the air, Merz caught the dragon by the tail. It thrashed and fought, trying to scorch him, but Merz pulled the dragon down close to his body with one arm, keeping its head facing away.

Bernie and Tish jumped onto Merz's outstretched arm as soon as they were close enough. Tish turned away when Merz broke the dragon's neck with his club, but Bernie watched in mingled horror and relief.

"Now, what about the lock?" Merz said, lifting his arm so he could hear them.

"We got it open. Well, Tish did," Bernie said.

"We did it together," said Tish, though she smiled gratefully at Bernie.

"It's open. Bernfried, Kagin, come help me open the portals," Merz shouted. Bernie and Tish had to cover their ears against the tremendous roar.

The two giants who had stood with Merz before broke off from their fight against the dragons and ran to help. One grabbed the lock and pulled it away, then dropped it and shook his hand. "It's scorching hot," he said.

"No time for hesitation," said Merz. He put the trolls down out of the way against the edge of the mountain. "Stay there," he said, adding "please" as an afterthought.

The three giants started to turn the giant winch, which opened the portals. High above them in the dark, it was as if three thin crescent moons appeared out of nowhere. Bernie and Tish stared up at the huge, gradually thickening crescents, but behind the giants, the dragons screeched as they saw the light.

"Stop them!" roared a dragon. Bernie recognized the voice of King Daranee.

The winch moved slowly, but as a wave of dragons descended on the three giants, bright rays of sunshine pierced through the openings.

"Tagatzur! Tagatzur!" The dragons fell into a panic and wheeled around, crashing into each other and the giants in their rush to get away from the opening as it grew wider and wider.

Soon, bright sunlight flooded into the mountain through the three huge round portals, illuminating the town, the wide empty areas outside the town, and all the way to the lairs where the dragons fled.

As the dragons flew away, the giants roared and stamped, and Bernie felt as if he would shake apart from the noise and rattling. He grabbed Tish, and the two hung on to each other as Merz danced and rejoiced with the others.

After the giants settled down, Merz remembered the trolls. "Let's get you two back to your parents," he said. Picking them up, he strode along. "I wish Fadz was here to see this," he said, a brief sadness crossing his face, "but I am glad to have avenged him. Never again will we let the dragons intimidate us."

Of course, wars never end so tidily. For the next three days, Bernie and the other trolls had to stay inside, as skirmishes broke out between the dragons and giants.

Since the dragons who had been exposed to sunlight could not breathe fire, the best they could do was dart in and attack with teeth and claws, then scramble away again. Still, one giant got a bad scratch on his eye, which would take a long time to heal, and another had to fight off several dragons at once and wound up with bites and scratches.

Overall though, the giants were able to control matters, and soon the trolls got restless. They knew there was a lot of cleanup and rebuilding to do at home, and they had a long walk back. At first, the grown-up trolls worried about finding their way, but Tish reminded her granny about the *langises* she left to mark their path. It took a while for Granny Mac to explain to the others, but they agreed if they traveled by day, the *langis* markers would be enough to guide them.

After the trolls decided it was time to leave, Bernie went to tell Merz. The giant listened, then nodded. "I'll miss you," he said, wiping his eyes, "but you've spent enough time here on our account." He smiled. "Still, there's time enough to have a feast!"

Later that evening, Merz brought the trolls a huge tub of water from a lake which lay near the mountain. It was filled with newts, water bugs and frogs, so the trolls prepared all their favorite dishes.

"How about a song to go with our food?" suggested Bernie's dad. Trolls love singing with their meals.

"Could you teach me one of yours?" asked Merz.

Bernie's dad rose to his feet.

"Your dad's going to sing," Tish called to Bernie, who was busy gobbling down frog sticks. "Hurry up." The two young trolls sat side by side, and Granny Mac and the other trolls joined them in a small circle. Merz leaned his head in close to hear better.

Bernie's dad cleared his throat. "I think we need a sharing song to celebrate sharing our meal with this illustrious giant, Merz." With that, he began.

Sing ho! for the meals, the wondrous meals
    We share with our friends - raise a glass!
    A cauldron of slugs spiced with beetles and eels
    Who cares if the eels give us gas?

Sing ho! for the water, which quenches our thirst
    For salamanders, sweet on the tongue
    For critters that skitter and bite, we're the worst
    We chomp them in half when we're stung.

But though we love eating, and eat till we groan
    Sharing our grub till the end
    Sharing's not fun if you do it alone,
    'Tis better to share with your friends!

The trolls cheered, and the giant clapped softly so as not to knock them down. Being polite, Bernie's mum offered Merz some newt stew and frog sticks, but while he thanked them profusely, he said he would stick to giant food.

After a full meal and more songs, the older trolls lay down to sleep. Bernie sat in the dark near the dying embers of the fire, listening to his mum and dad snore and thinking about his adventures. He got up and walked to where he could see the moon peeking over the edge of the open portal above.

As he gazed up, he felt a prickling feeling as if he were being watched. He turned, thinking Tish might have had trouble sleeping as well, but there in the dark were two gleaming eyes, and the air had a sudden bitter taste he'd thought he'd left behind.

"I hoped I might find you here," hissed a voice he recognized. It was Mionaa. "You think you're so clever, but there are no giants around to protect you now."

Bernie backed slowly away, but the dragon princess followed him, getting closer and closer. "Help," he cried, but it came out in a squeak that wouldn't have woken a mouse, much less a giant.

"Squeak away, little troll," said Mionaa. "There's nobody to help you."

"You're wrong, dragon. He's got me."

Mionaa twisted her head to see Tish. She stared, and then chuckled deep in her throat. "How wonderful, your *girlfriend* is here to save you. She'll make a tasty dessert after I eat you up."

"Run, Tish, run," shouted Bernie, finding his voice at last, but Mionaa reached out and grabbed Tish by the leg.

"Now, shall I toast you first or eat you raw?" she asked in a nasty voice.

"You… you can't breathe fire anymore. The, er, sunlight…" stammered Bernie, trying to distract the dragon while he looked around for some way to rescue Tish.

"Ah, but that's where you're wrong." Mionaa let Tish go, and as the girl dashed toward Bernie, she let out a puff of fire, only a tiny puff, but it burned Tish, who rolled on the ground to put out the flame. "Daddy was so protective of his little girl, he made me stay back in the caves during the battle. I never flew into the sunshine, so I can still breathe fire."

"I'm going to pay you back for what you did to us," she snarled. "Let's see how you laugh at dragons when your skin is burned off and your insides are roasted."

SOMETHING TASTY

REARING BACK AS IF TO UNLEASH A MIGHTY FLAME TOWARD THEM, Mionaa instead yelped and jerked as Bernie's mum and dad leaped out of the darkness from either side and landed on her wings. She twisted to scratch with her sharp talons, but before she could, the three other trolls from Bernie's town clambered up and held her down.

"Let me go," she shouted, her snout pressed against the ground by their weight so she couldn't breathe fire at them.

"No chance, princess," said Granny Mac, limping into view.

Bernie laughed as his mum called out, "Are you all right, dear?"

"I'm fine, mum," he said, walking over to help Tish to her feet.

"Should we kill her, son?" Bernie's dad asked, with an air of respect and deference Bernie had never heard before.

The question silenced them all as they held down the struggling dragon, but Bernie shook his head. "There have been enough who've been hurt and killed. I have a better idea."

It took all the trolls to pull and prod Mionaa over to the cages, and she managed to let off a few fiery spurts they barely avoided. At last, they got her crowded into the wooden cage where the horses had been. She had to curl up to fit, but they got the door closed and locked.

"You'll be safe in here until morning," said Bernie to the angry but subdued dragon, "but I wouldn't breathe any fire if I were you. It would only light the cage on fire, and we couldn't get you out again."

"You'll regret this, troll," hissed Mionaa, but her voice sounded thin and scared, and she said no more.

The trolls moved well away from Mionaa's cage to sleep. Granny Mac helped Tish with her burned back while Bernie yawned and yawned. When Tish was finally settled, Bernie gave a last huge yawn and lay down himself. He was asleep before his head touched the ground.

A bright ray of sunshine woke Bernie. For a moment, he couldn't figure out where he was and how the sun had reached him, but then he remembered how the giants opened the portal. He looked around, amazed at the expanse of the huge cavern. Light shone on the ruins of other buildings far from the giant's town, and there was even a castle off in the distance, which looked like it had fallen in on itself in some distant age.

"I see you had a visitor," boomed Merz, walking up from town and picking up the cage to stare at Mionaa. "We should have guarded you better, though it looks like you were able to handle things quite well on your own. I never thought much of trolls, I doubt any of us did, but I don't think we'll underestimate you again. As for this young dragon, I'll be sure she gets back to her father, who is probably worried sick about her. Perhaps her return will help prove we mean them no harm so long as they leave us alone."

Bernie agreed, but he had more pressing concerns. "I'm glad

we could help, but we need to be getting home. There's a lot of cleaning up we have to do."

Merz blushed. "I'm sorry for the mess we made. We owe you all a great debt, and would be happy to help you rebuild, though…" He didn't go on, but looked embarrassed.

"We don't need help rebuilding," piped up Bernie's dad. "I mean to say, thank you, but trolls don't usually build things either, at least not our kind. I think we might have someone who could help us." He reached out a burly arm and patted a surprised Tish on the head. "I think maybe we underestimated this young lady, but if she were willing to help…"

"Oh, I'd love to," Tish gushed. "Why, I think I have an idea now. When we were traveling to Mount Dreadful, Bernie rescued me with a special trick, and we might be able to use a similar trick to build a bridge."

Bernie's ears felt like they might burn up, but he smiled at Tish.

"See, we have two young trolls with something to teach us," said Bernie's mum proudly, and Granny Mac and the others agreed. "But there is something you could do for us, Mr. Giant," she went on.

"It's Merz, mum," Bernie whispered to her. "His name is Merz."

"Mr. Merz," she said, "could you give us a lift back home? It's a long way back, and I'm eager to get there, though you might want to leave us at the edge of our forest. Otherwise, you might frighten the other trolls." She looked at Bernie and whispered back, "Sometimes even grown-up trolls get scared."

Merz leaned way over and tipped his hat to the trolls. "It would be an honor."

With that, he held out his arms, and Bernie, Tish and Granny Mac climbed up and sat on his shoulders, gripping his hair to keep from falling off. If it hurt any, Merz didn't let on. He called to Kagin and Bernfried, who stood outside, and the three giants carried the trolls up, out of the mountain, and across the plains. As they strode across the land, Bernie and Tish pointed out places they had stopped on their way.

"I wonder if the *langises* are still there," Tish said suddenly.

"We don't need them now," Bernie pointed out. The giants know where they are going.

"Yes," said Tish, "but what if we want to visit the giants again?"

Bernie nodded. "I'm sure they'll still be there when we are ready," he said. "Besides, Granny Mac would probably come along to help us find our way."

Granny Mac nodded.

When they reached the edge of the pine forest, the three giants stopped and said goodbye.

Merz leaned over and shook Bernie's hand, or rather his whole arm. "If there is ever anything we can do to repay you, let us know. You and Tish and your families are always welcome in Jötunheimr." Then he winked at Bernie. "And if we ever need help again, we'll know who to call."

As the giants strode away, Bernie's mum and dad stood beside him and waved at the giants. For a long time, Bernie felt the thud thud thud of the giants' footsteps, and the faint bittersweet scent of goodbyes hung in the air.

"They are something, aren't they?" said Bernie's mum. "I still can't believe we got out of that mess without being eaten." She rubbed Bernie's head and pulled on his ears. "Speaking of which," she laughed, "it's been a long time since we ate. Maybe you and Tish could find us some lizards or beetles to munch on."

"I'll bet I find some first," yelled Tish, and the two young trolls trotted off to tip over rocks and look for something tasty.

ACKNOWLEDGMENTS

Many thanks to Stephanie Taylor at Clean Reads for recognizing and believing in my story, and to my editors, Christi Corbett, Leslie Grant, and Jaime Powell, for your keen eyes and caring attention.

To all my fellow authors who read and re-read my words even when they tumbled out disjointed and incoherent. Somehow, you still managed to give me great insight, feedback, and encouragement.

To my long time writing friends from Writing.com who have been there from the beginning, especially Breanna Teintze, whose support and feedback have been endless and invaluable. Also to Breanna's daughter, Rosie, who will always hold the title First Reader.

To my stalwart writing group at Mac's Back on Coventry, who have supported me through hesitation, frustration, and jubilation. You have kept it real and kept me sane. (Well, at least you tried.)

To my parents, who shared their deep love of reading and adventure with me and my brothers. To my mother-in-law, Ruth Langhinrichs, who has inspired and encouraged me. To my grandmother, whose faith in me stays with me always. To my three children, who have patiently supported my writing, poetry, and stories (even though they roll their eyes at my jokes).

To the authors who created wonderful worlds for me to visit when I was young, especially C.S. Lewis, J.R.R. Tolkien, and L. Frank Baum. Also to the authors who reminded me that more wonderful worlds remain to be created, notably J.K. Rowling, Eva Ibbotson, and Liesl Shurtliff, but so many more I can't name.

Finally, more thanks and love than I can ever express to my wife, Julie, who has stood by me, encouraged me, and believed in me even when I didn't always believe in myself.

"Suppose we have only dreamed, or made up, all those things- trees and grass and sun and moon and stars and Aslan himself. Suppose we have. Then all I can say is that, in that case, the made-up things seem a good deal more important than the real ones." – Puddleglum, in C.S. Lewis' *The Silver Chair*

ABOUT THE AUTHOR

Ben Langhinrichs lives a peaceful life in Shaker Heights, Ohio with his wife and cats, and an occasional whirlwind visit by one of his three grown children and their loved ones. Since childhood, he has spent countless hours lost in Narnia, Middle Earth, and the Land of Oz, returning to our world only long enough for snacks and the occasional long walk. When he isn't reading or writing fantastical adventures for young people, he writes software for his slightly magical business, Genii Software.

Although *Danger Tastes Dreadful* is his first novel, he is hard at work on a sequel in which Bernie and Tish tumble down to the Treacherous Sea and encounter biting eels, enchanting mertrolls, and giant fire wasps.

You can visit him online at BenLanghinrichs.net or say hello on Twitter @blanghinrichs.

www.cleanreads.com

CPSIA information can be obtained
at www.ICGtesting.com
Printed in the USA
BVHW03s1316091018
529695BV00001B/31/P